MÉLANGE

Musings on Life from a Writer's Pen

Janie P. Bess

www.melangewrc.com

MÉLANGE

Musings on Life from a Writer's Pen

A Compilation by the
Writers Resource Center
of Northern California

MICAH 6:8
BOOKS

Mélange: Musings on Life from a Writer's Pen
Writers Resource Center of Northern California

Copyright © 2018

Published by W.B. Campbell Publications/Micah 6:8 Books

First Printing October 2018

ISBN 10: 0-9897968-6-8
ISBN 13: 978-0-9897968-6-6

Library of Congress Control Number: 2018906741

Cover Concept/Design: Tywebbin Creations and WRC

Printed in the United States

Foreword

Writers Resource Center began in the most unorthodox way. I was a hairstylist near Travis Air Force Base in Fairfield, California. That's how I discovered my new calling: story-telling. My clients loved to hear about my experiences as a military wife living in Asia. One client, Pam, convinced me to write a book. She swore, it was because of my stories, she found the will to fight for her autistic son's education.

During spring break, Pam visited my home and met my family: my husband, David Sr, son, little David, daughter, Terri, and our youngest son, Tony. Pam found it hard to believe little David was deaf and blind as he walked around the house doing chores as though he could see. When he felt her presence, little David walked over to her and placed her hands in his and began to teach her the letters of the alphabet using tactile sign language. Pam was even more amazed when he went into the laundry room and returned with a basketful of clean clothes to fold. Her mouth flew open, in disbelief, as he folded towels into neat uniformed squares before stacking them in the linen closet nearby.

I explained, "Little David does not know he is handicapped. He's exceptionally smart and independent." Pam encouraged me to write a book about David. She felt my story would be an encouragement and give hope to mothers whose children were physically challenged. Before Pam moved back to Ohio, she committed to sending me information about the Writer's Digest Correspondence School and made me promise to write my story. Within a few weeks, I received the information promised, plus a fully paid scholarship.

I kept my promise. My instructor at Writers Digest recommended I find a local writers' group to help me learn computer skills. I found a writers' group, but I was snubbed. They told me, my story should be fiction because no one would want to read a Black version of Helen Keller. I left totally embarrassed.

I met Bud Gardner in Fairfield's Barnes & Noble bookstore and traveled 40 miles to attend his writing workshop in Sacramento, California. Nine months later, I completed the course. The long trips made me sleepy in class, so Bud advised me to find a group near home. I told him what happened with the writers in town, and he said, "Why don't you just start your own?"

I had big dreams. I wanted more than the typical small group of writers gathering once a month for critique. I also wanted to attract experienced authors who could present classes like Bud Gardner's, but on a larger scale. February 2002, Danette Mitchell and I went to work to promote a local writers' group. We attended every Chamber of Commerce meeting, joining three. We announced our plans for the largest writers' conference in Northern California.

Danette, as a technical writer, designed fliers, wrote sponsorship letters, and with my wild ideas, invited local writers for a luncheon at my house. Fifty people showed up. Our first official meeting at our local Barnes and Noble went well. *New York Times* bestselling authors volunteered to hold free workshops for our newly formed group. We made history hosting the first-ever writers' conference in Solano County at the Holiday Inn. It was amazing! Over 300 attendees showed up and over 150 people signed up for memberships.

With my husband's blessing and financial support, Writers Resource Center of Northern California was birthed on October 8, 2003 as a 501c3 Non-profit. WRC has seen many changes over the years, mainly combining three chapters established throughout Northern California into one. Many have joined WRC as aspiring writers, and became award-winning published authors. It all began, because I kept my promise to Pam to tell David's story. My first book, *Visions* was published with the help of WRC. This year we are celebrating fifteen years of writing, learning, and developing.

On my first day on the job as Cosmetology Instructor at Le' Mélange Beauty College/Salon in

Napa, California, I fell in love with the fancy name. Out of curiosity, I asked the owner how to pronounce the name and what it meant. She explained that mélange is a French word meaning a mixture, combination or assortment of words, things, like a medley of colorful flowers, an assortment of whatever like mish-mash. Our beauty students were just that — a mixture of different nationalities, and assorted skin tones with colorful personalities to boot.

Mélange: Musings on Life from a Writer's Pen, reminds me of those beauty students from countries like India, Japan, Nigeria, and Puerto Rico. Mélange is the perfect title for WRC's first anthology. Our members are a mélange of nationalities, backgrounds, and cultures. Our ages span from the young, to the seasoned to the young at heart; from novices to veteran writers. We have mothers, fathers, grandparents, teachers, ministers, doctors, high school and college students. Each of us brings a unique fragrance and we are united by our love for writing.

Mélange: Musings on Life from a Writer's Pen will warm your heart, make you laugh and shed a tear, as our members share their hearts and experiences. The stories and poems may even challenge your way of thinking with simplistic and controversial themes. Mélange is a mish-mash of muses. Whatever stage life finds you, you will find yourself in this anthology.

Moreover, *Mélange: Musings on Life from a Writer's Pen* is the manifestation of a dream, the birth of a passion, and the building block for great things to come!

Read, enjoy, and be inspired.

Janie P Bess,
Founder, Writers Resource Center
of Northern California

Contents

MÉLANGE

Musings on Life from a Writer's Pen

Southern Born

By Carole Morrison

I don't reckon I will get over being southern, or that I would want to.

It's the people. Southern people got manners. Even if they quit school in the 7th grade and went to work as a mill hand, they know how to say "Please" and "thank you" and "Yes, ma'am" and "No, ma'am". And to let old people go first.

It's the place, too. Where I was born. It's Georgia red clay. Once it gets on you, nothing will take it off. Humidity that wilts your hair and takes your breath away and makes Yankee women sweat and southern women glisten.

It's "Amazing Grace" drifting out of Ebenezer Baptist Church on Sunday mornings. "I once was lost—oh, yes, Lord, but now I'm found. Thank you, Jesus. Was blind, but now I see," and it's the spirit of my people who were here eight generations before I was born.

It's Papa on the front porch of the little cement block house in his rocking chair. Pouch of pipe tobacco on his knee, rocking and smoking the night away. Some nights he would take out his harmonica and blow some blues.

It's Mama in her hand-me-down dresses from her rich sister up in New York feeding the stray cats, and sweeping the bare floor and cooking up turnip greens, blackeye peas, and a cake of cornbread dripping with sweet cream butter.

It's Great Uncle Robert riding the highway from Rome to Valdosta "tending to the sick folk". The widowed sister with no children to look after her. The oldest sister who took in a grandchild to raise. A brother with a bad heart. All elderly now. All in need of one thing or another and waiting for Robert to take care of them.

I heard Uncle Robert was bad to run around on his wife with other women, but he brought me a warm winter coat, and when I was twelve, he and his wife took me to the first cafe I had ever been to.

Great Aunt Susie married a policeman. He shot a man during a robbery, then shot himself to death in the outhouse. They said he couldn't get over killing a man even if he did rob a bank. Susie cried all the way to the grave until Mama reminded her of the women he had up at the Kimball House Hotel.

My first cousin, Billy, lost his daddy when he was three to tuberculosis, and his stepdaddy beat him a lot. Billy served in the United States Coast Guard, got out and took his GED test for a high school diploma, and ended up an executive vice president of a big company up in Atlanta.

Most of my cousins didn't make it though. Some got sidelined by drugs and alcohol or a bad woman, or no-account man, and some just didn't seem to want to do better.

Annie took to drugs and drinking. She lived on the street and up and died young. Frank had some trouble with the law over a stolen car and went to the state prison. Sue took a lot of acid and no one knows what happened to her after her daddy and mama died and couldn't take care of her anymore. I loved them all.

My daddy got asked to leave Daniel C. O'Keefe High School in the tenth grade for fighting, but when he was twenty he was broadcasting the news over WSB radio in Atlanta, an NBC affiliate.

When I was five, Daddy left the mess of his young marriage and went on to news broadcasting up north. He said he would come back to get me someday and he did. When I was fifteen and too wild for my grandparents to handle, he took me to California. He said I had to go to school. And I did. I finished and got me a good job teaching school. I owe that to my daddy.

I have lived far away from Georgia for longer than I ever lived there, but I can't shake it off. I tried to lose my southern accent because people thought I was ignorant, but it stuck. I said I was from Georgia, and people in California would correct me and say "Jaw-Ja" and I never could figure that out.

Most of my people are gone now. Some were good men and women, and some were not. We went through a lot together. We had great joy, and crushing sorrow. Stupifying failure and stunning success.

I would not have wanted to be born anywhere else to any other people.

The Mannequins
By Carl Weber

The strangest times
Of just simple breath
Begging...for a sound of life.
Times when
An eternal numbness
Seems the answer.
Just the lonely are lucky.
Asking...where am I?
A scene which merely fades away.

A great grand slowing down
To a mere stare.
A quiet breathing breath.
To a moment when ears hear
Only breath, only breath, only air,
Ingoing and out
And THIS is life.

How best not to feel, not to think,
To adore the quiet silence.
Yes and only yes,
The best of minds know well
The sanitarium.

The strangest times of breath
When all the quiet is done.
When breath no longer breathes.
How lucky...the brain dead.
How lucky...the mannequins.

The Benefits of Discomfort
By Vicki Ward

Don't you like being comfortable? Who doesn't? Everyone talks about getting comfortable with life. Comfort is something we're taught to want and seek throughout life. So what does comfort really mean? Those who run toward obstacles, who court danger, and are thrilled by the unknown, are considered quirky, at best. To be comfortable suggests you may not have to sacrifice. You may have an easy road to travel with fewer obstacles to jump over, or work around. These could include clingy needy friends, who are always trying to get out of a jam, or that friend who always needs to borrow a few dollars until payday, which never seems to come.

These days I seem to find myself short with friends. My man may as well wait until I'm in bed dosed with a glass or two of wine nursing my mood before he tries to come close. Something is wrong in my world, yet I don't have a clue what it is. I finally *heard* my sister! Yes, the one who always talks too much and makes sure I heard it from her. She has walked around my house chiming in over and over so much, I easily tuned her out. My insults and ignoring did nothing to silence her.

One morning, I woke up to the truth of her words, along with a rip-roaring headache. My first conscious thought was how right she was. Through hazy thoughts I remembered having drinks and too much conversation about change the previous night. Her words now rang true, surprising me. She was right, and I now knew it! Her voice was still ringing in my ears. Her truths could not be denied. Yes, I had become so comfortable I was miserable, yet didn't realize it.

I had defied my mother and grandmother in this with other hard and fast beliefs I set for myself. Comfort was something I sought and I now can see was ultimately the source of my discontent. I looked around the room, feeling lost and adrift. To admit I had these feelings that I harbored and denied existed was disappointing to me. No, not me! I began to recall life lessons my mom and grandmother doled out when I was young.

I was stubborn, and didn't agree with their *old* logic. I learned my quick mouth would get me into trouble. I quietly shut my mouth so I would not get it smacked shut, if I attempted to challenge them. I always remembered hearing about getting comfortable in bed, feeling comfortable in new jeans, and many other comfortable issues, so in my mind I wanted that too, and simply could not agree with the concept of not being comfortable.

As far as I was concerned, I couldn't get comfortable soon enough! I had watched my mom wok her ass off, after my dad died just to keep a roof over her, me and my sister's heads. The fatigue she wore covered her face, weakened her knees, and bent her back. Looking back, I realized she never really talked about how tired she was, if she wanted to quit her job, or needed more rest. She might come home and make the statement, but never lingered.

Replaying things my sister had been driving home for far too long, I realized the misery I was suffering from was that I had gotten too comfortable with — my life, my husband, my job, and my family, and that had become my torment. I really thought I had a handle on life, and believed for the longest time that if I was comfortable, that's all that mattered. That's what I wanted. I became fixed on the idea of comfort being the only thing to strive for, and discarded the notion I really needed anything more. I realized I was afraid of challenges, and as long as I stayed where I felt comfortable, I was fine.

I knew I needed some help to understand and completely accept this new revolution. Sis had often given me notes, and the names of books to read, and websites to visit, that I routinely rejected. I took out a pad and began to write, flooded with thoughts. I wrote down titles like what was good in my life and why, and started listing things under each title. On another page I wrote a title of what was not good and why it wasn't, and began listing my life issues under each one.

I had to keep writing, no time to question. Gut-wrenching pain had me in tears as I listed and answered questions about the relationship I had with my husband. Other pages included my house, my job, my family, my friends. At times I could barely see the paper for the steady stream of tears interrupting my writing. I refused to stop, afraid if I did I would never return to this gut- wrenching task. I wiped my eyes, nose, and my pages of truth with Kleenex and soldiered on.

I went to the kitchen just long enough to get a cup of coffee, and returned to the room, determined. Never had I experienced such a rush of emotions, such a torrent of self-involved crying, yet also experienced the drain of oppression, the drain of lifelessness, and the implant of openness, and hope. I decided to get bolder, and a bit sheepish. I wrote my new expectations for family, job, house and husband, and could not stop.

The task was much too large to finish that morning. I needed to research information to assist me with this journey, which I shared with absolutely no one. I wanted to share with my husband and my sister, but was fearful of what they would say or think, and of what I would do, say or think about their comments. No, this journey of liberation needed to be understood by me before I began to open the window to others about new thoughts and ideas both opening me to gaining more comfort in my life.

I learned that comfort is severely underrated, and that we only *grow through discomfort*. I learned that we will always want just what we have if we do not stretch ourselves. We are created for challenge, built for change. We cannot achieve some of the simplest, and of course the greatest life challenges if we do not become aware of and react to being uncomfortable. This is something natural and to be expected.

Over time I learned this and so much more about the condition of life and the real me. I can see just how much I missed out on because I didn't want to be challenged, and fail. Challenges, failures, successes, life lessons, developing relationships where you may be on either side of the comfort line are all inherent with life. They are all wrapped up in the unique entity of life. I am thankful for being allowed to know, understand and welcome being uncomfortable.

Journey Beneath the Bay
A BART Episode of Enduring Consequence
by Linda Dogué Holliman

Bay Area Rapid Transit, the Bay Area's commuter
train system known as BART, is more to me than
just a convenient means of transportation. One mem-
orable night over twenty years ago, deep within the
barnacled Transbay Tube firmly anchored to the
bottom of the San Francisco Bay, seated on a BART
train speeding toward The City, my Prince Charming
and I became engaged.

We sat across from each other nestled in the facing
seats at the front end of a middle car. I was traveling backward, he forward. Steel wheels repeated a
high-pitched refrain and lights on the tunnel walls
whizzed across the car's picture windows as the
train rocketed through.

A couple of rows behind my guy in the near-empty
car, an elderly lady seemed to be doing her best not
to be intrusive. Her soft smile and circumspect
gaze conveyed that she was a willing witness to

our tender scene and that she gave her full approval. Her comforting eyes, her brown cheeks...she very much resembled my maternal grandmother...right down to her beauty shop hairdo and her matronly coat. Next to her, at attention, I noticed the upright handles of a paper shopping bag. I could not see her handbag or sensible shoes, but I knew they were there hidden in their places beyond my new fiancé's seatback. My grandmother never had a chance to meet my intended...heart problems....This lovely lady observing us was my grandmother's proxy that night, and thus the first member of my family to learn of our exciting news.

And so it was, that as that BART train rolled on beneath the San Francisco Bay, my fiancé figuratively traveled forward into his new future, and I looked back in adieu to my past.

When I replay the video on my mind's screen, the camera parallels the train. At first moving along the elevated tracks, passing the fanciful Gingerbread House Restaurant and the indomitable Oakland Main Post Office, I see the exterior of the silvery white train with its familiar blue markings bathed in moonlight. Framed by the car's windows, I see a young couple in love leaning in toward each other, a silent sentry seated close by behind the young man. The next scene shows the train plunging into the darkness of the Transbay Tube. In the final scene, the railcar emerges from the underwater tunnel into the subterranean Embarcadero Station in San Francisco. A double blast of its electric horn heralds the arrival of the newly affianced couple. The announcement produces no congratulations, for neither the train operator nor any BART officials are aware of what has just taken place within their jurisdiction. The elderly lady alone has shared this life-changing moment with the two young people.

Hand in hand, the young couple step from the train onto the platform, crossing the threshold into their new life together. The young man's voice quavers under the weight of his new responsibility. What just happened? He boarded the train single and carefree, traversed the underwater portal, and emerged a practically married man! The young woman smiles, radiant with joy. The elderly lady continues on her trip, for the time being, forgotten by the elated young woman. And there my movie ends.

For the past twenty some years, every BART trip to San Francisco with my spouse becomes a renewal of our engagement commitment. As the train descends into the Tube, I become as giddy as a little girl at Macy's hopping up and down at the counter while her mom pays for her new party dress. My husband tells me he would marry me all over again. I tell him I am inexpressibly content that I am his wife. My heart races as fast as the train. BART is our own personal Disneyland ride.

When our teenaged sons accompany us, accessorized with smart phones and earbuds, they look obliquely at their dad and me with a public show of disapproval, and roll their eyes in unison. When they were younger, they were entertained by our fairytale. I know that they are obligated to feign teenage disinterest, but I also know that the epic deeds of their mutual hero, their dad, are well-woven into the thick fabric of their lives.

BART is a golden treasure to me. Like my engagement and wedding rings, BART is an enduring symbol of the love and life I share with a most amazing man.

Little Lottie Ant

By Anita L. Robertson

News spread quickly of the deserted picnic site. The scout ant had barely been able to relay the location coordinates to her supervisor before jubilation broke out in the hungry ant colony. Within seconds, thousands of ants ascended from their quarters deep within the ground, their bodies, a glistening carpet of movement reflecting a sea of amber sunshine. A call was shouted, "Workers assemble."

Little Lottie Ant turned to her mother upon exiting the corridor tube and with her body bouncing yelled, "I want to go too! Please let me go."

"I don't think you're quite ready yet, Lottie. We've only practiced your pheromone tracking a few times."

"But, Mom, you said I was really, really, good at it—a natural. Pleeease?"

"Well, I don't know," said her mother, tilting her head.

"I promise, I'll make sure there aren't any gaps! Pleeease? I'm old enough. Even Jenny's mom said she could go the next time there was a food run."

"Well...well, okay, Lottie. Just make sure you keep your antennae pointed forward at all times," her voice gripped by apprehension.

Before her mother could change her mind, Lottie was gone, swept into the parade of the worker ants. Lottie quickly found a place in the single-file procession in front of a more mature female, who upon seeing Lottie, commented to her larger friend, "Some ants still belong in the nursery."

I can do as much as anybody, and even more, Lottie thought, and set forth with greater conviction and confidence when the order to march was cried out.

The group travelled to the site quickly; it was necessary to get back before the energy of the sun would be lost and their bodies significantly slowed. They had traversed over moss covered logs and under decaying leaves, around large trees and rocks of every size, and before Lottie knew it, the forest floor had given way to an open meadow. The breeze was gusty, and the smell of human food wafted past the disciplined ants. As Lottie got closer to the front of the shortening line, she could see the point where each ant broke rank and set forth in its own limited direction. She jumped up and down, her antennae dancing in the air.

"Little ant," the familiar voice jeered from behind, "I see a few crumbs you can get." Lottie grew red, and before she had time to retort, she was at the front of the line, the turbulence of the bodies driving her to the outer boundary of the retrieval area. Remembering what her mother had taught her, Lottie reached up with her antennae and started to consciously taste the air. She caught the impression of a food source situated a short distance away, deducing that it was quite large and worth the forage to acquire it. Quickly running toward the aroma, she found the edible to be triangle-shaped and multi-layered. It had a top and bottom which were white and spongy and an inner layer that was thin, dark and dense with a pungent yellow material that, she concluded, could not possibly be food. In fact, the yellow substance so wreaked havoc on Lottie's senses, that she found it hard to get her bearings. But, after running around the edible several times, clarity ensued, and she was able to resolve the best way to hoist and balance it, and carefully did so. With the heavy prize barely secure, Lottie gingerly set forth to find the pheromone trail that would lead her back to the retrieval site. However, the descending sun had chased away the wind and the acrid cloud of the yellow substance surrounded her, impairing her senses again.

"I think this is the trail. Yes, it must be!" she stated and proceeded onward. "Won't everyone be so impressed when they see me bring this back? Those big ants can...Whoa!" Having not kept her antennae forward, Lottie found herself in a hole, under complete darkness. The edible covered her view of the tangerine sky. Tears of confusion and humility mixed as she sat pondering her situation.

"What shall I do? What shall I do?" echoed her voice through the desolate chamber. It became clear that the home was deserted as it smelled of stale mole.

"You should eat," responded a pleasant voice from deep within the edible.

"We have plenty here," added a second.

"Where are you? Who are you?" Lottie replied.

"We are here inside the nourishment center. The brown matter is delicious, we've been eating it for days now."

The second voice added, "I'm Bly and my sister is Sky. We are maggots—very content ones indeed."

"Oh, pleased to meet you. I'm Lottie, Lottie Ant."

"Come on in and join us, Lottie"

"I would love to, but I have to get back to my group before they leave without me." And with that, Lottie crawled up the side of the hole, lifted her front legs, and gave a hard push on the tightly wedged edible. The white matter gave way slightly but then bounced back. She tried again.

"Ugh! I can't move it! How am I gonna get out of here?"

"We don't know, all we can think about is eating!" said Bly.

Lottie lit up. "Do you think you can eat out a tunnel for me?"

"Sure. Just make yourself comfortable and tell us a few stories. Otherwise, it may be a long two days," said Sky.

"What! I don't have two days, I need to leave now," yelled Lottie in a panic.

"I'm sorry, but we have gotten so full-figured that we can barely move." said Bly.

"Oh, the satisfaction of gorging! We shall make beautiful flies!" responded Sky.

Hanging her head in despair, Lottie became conscious of the cold permeating her exoskeleton. "Sticks and stones will break my home, but the cold will never hurt me. Sticks and stones...Hey! I have an idea." With antenna held high, Lottie fastidiously began searching for small sticks and as the home was dilapidated, she was able to find some with relative ease. With her load, she again scrambled up the side of the hole and carefully placed the end of one stick against the hole's wall and the other end into the spongy edible, creating a gap. She continued with the other sticks until she had effectively created a narrow opening through which she could squeeze. With relief and the effects of a small amount of sunlight warming her body, she yelled, "Good-bye" through the top of the spongy edible to the two confused maggots and began to retrace her steps.

After finding her initial directional error and correcting it, Lottie proceeded back to the group's retrieval site, only to find it had been scavenged clean and that her comrades were gone. Because the way home had been so strongly marked by the collective, Lottie knew that she would not get lost. However, explaining her delay to her mother would be a problem.

"She's gonna make me tend the pupae. I'm gonna die of boredom," she thought and with that she ran as the sun started to descend under its blanket of green. Lottie felt her body slowing down as she made her way past the familiar obstacles of the macro landscape. Emerging from under a fallen leaf, her sensitive antennae caught the taste of a nearby treat, its sweetness amplified by the increasing dampness of the forest air. She stopped, torn between continuing home or discovering where the beckoning treasure lie. Home could wait she concluded as she decisively stepped off the marked trail and meandered through a plethora of ferns where a little aphid peeked its head from around a stem and smiled.

"Hi," said the aphid.

"Hi. My name is Lottie, what's your name?"

"I'm Alice," she replied, her smile growing larger. "Are you an ant?"

"Yes, I am. I could taste honeydew and I traced it here, to you. It's irresistible! Actually, I can sense even more now, over there," she said lifting two of her legs to show the aphid.

"Oh, that must be coming from my family. I got separated from them a long time ago and now I'm stuck here. Can you help me get back?"

Lottie could see tears forming in Alice's eyes, and knowing firsthand what it felt like to be alone, she did not hesitate to help. She quickly sprinted up the fern stalk and nestled the aphid in her arms, descended, and set out in the direction of Alice's family.

The aphid colony was only two plants away and it took no time for Lottie to place her new friend back onto her family's fern stem. Alice's family of ninety-eight were so overjoyed to have Alice back that they showered Lottie with gratitude.

"Please, take some honeydew back to your nest and let your queen know that we are here," said Alice's mother, giving Lottie a hug, which produced some of the sugary gift.

"Thank you, I will let them know," Lottie replied. She could feel no warmth on her body and knew she had to head home immediately. She followed her steps back to the main trail and slowly made her way back.

When Lottie arrived at the nest, a voice called out from the darkness of the lookout, "Incoming ant" whereupon she was immediately surrounded by soldier ants. As she had no security clearance to be out by herself or late at night, she was immediately escorted down an extra-wide tunnel to the queen, who was sitting on a hosta leaf overlooking the chamber.

"You must be our little missing ant, Lottie," said the queen upon seeing the dirty ant.

"Yes...yes, I am," Lottie replied trying to catch her breath.

"What happened to you, my dear?" the queen continued. "We have all been worried."

Lottie cleared her throat. "I found a large edible... then I got stuck in a hole...then I found an aphid, Alice, who I took home...and her mom gave me this," she said, producing the drop of honeydew. "It's for you, she said."

The queen's eyes widened upon sensing the treat and the formerly sleepy bodyguards now held their bodies straight and alert.

"Were there any other ants present at this aphid site? The queen waited for Lottie's answer, her strong antennae moving wildly.

"No," answered Lottie.

"Thank you, Lottie, I am glad you are home safe." With that she nodded to the guards who carefully escorted Lottie back into her mother's care.

The next day, news of Lottie's adventure had spread. Some had reacted with admiration, others with sympathy, and still others with horror. But it was the queen's statement that was the most antici-pated and it would be delivered at sunset.

"Will Lottie be punished? How? Will the queen be lenient? Is she happy?" they whispered.

As the sun begin to set, the call for assembly was announced. Lottie and her mother joined the multi-tudes that stood waiting for the queen, their antennae moving about like the waves of a turbulent ocean. With the queen's entrance the movement stopped, all eyes fixed above on the drooping branch of a maple sapling, waiting for her words. Lottie's heart was racing. She was sure everyone could hear it.

"My loyal subjects, as you have all heard by now, Lottie was lost last evening but is now safe. For that we are all grateful. I have summoned you all here to bring you up to date on developments that have since transpired since her return. This morning, I sent out a scout to confirm the existence of an aphid colony that appeared in need of our protection services. I am pleased to say that this was indeed confirmed."

Loud cheers rang out and ant bodies jumped about in celebration.

The queen waited for the excitement to subside then continued. "We will now have a steady source of food and we have Little Lottie to thank for this. Lottie has shown that she possesses great resourcefulness, perseverance and courage. These are the qualities that are necessary to be a successful scout. I hereby grant Lottie Ant entrance into our Elite Scout Unit of Ants, effective immediately. Congratulations, Lottie. And now I will make the necessary arrangements for a feast that is so long overdue. Assembly adjourned."

Loud cheers rang out again and Lottie felt relief then pride. She had proven herself to the colony; her determination had paid off.

Stolen Eraser
by Grant Holliman

I'm black. I was accused of stealing my friend's eraser and thought that was racist because my white friends weren't accused. I didn't even sit by the guy, but all the white kids did, and he blamed me! I was the one who stole his eraser, but that's beside the point. I was wrongly accused. I only stole his eraser because he stole it from me. And I accused him of stealing it from me because he's black.

Walking Unexpected Treasures
By Rita "em" Emery

An early morning walk on the trail of the East
    Bay Regional Park...
No better way to view the green hills, wild
    flowers, along
With eye-popping surprises that hum with life.

A bend in the trail makes for a slight turn
    to the left
There stands the most majestic deer ever seen
Become motionless...intrigued by the sight.

Further down the trail a bobcat spotted or
Was it a cougar or coyote disappearing into
    the thicket...
So quick, just a speck to the eye...nevertheless, the
    conclusion unknown.

Glancing at the fit bit watch...suddenly a snake
    slithers slowly across the trail...
Regardless of fear...passed the test...not
    going totally
Berserk with both feet still on the ground,
    heart intact.

Feet heavy from uneven, crumbly earth...head
    back...leaves rattling in a breeze
Ground squirrels, lizards, jack rabbits, quail
    scurrying about
Busy as can be or...just goofing off.

Only sounds within vicinity of the entrance, birds
    chirping away...
Even for the briefest moment...all was
    unexpected viewing...
Makes for an awesome inspiring walk away from
    the hustle and bustle of life.

The Winning Key
By Steven R. Butler

We all have at one time or another mused over how just one tiny change would make us happy. If I were only taller, shorter, slimmer, richer, smarter, sexier, or younger. And how many times have we wished, oh, if I could only win the lottery.

When we think of the extreme odds of Super Lotto, that concept most often fades away into a pipe dream, a daydream meant for another day. But I've never thought of the lottery as chance. I believe that it is all about fortune, of the universe sending us a well-needed message.

And with that thought, I'll recall my own experience, a game we knew back in the day as Mayor Art's Key Ring Contest.

I was 8 years old in the summer of 1959, just out of the second grade. Those were the summers that seemed to last for an eternity. I would spend the three months, between the last days of school in June and the first of the new school year in

September, in my own little world at our home on Deer Park Road in St. Helena, the summer days seemingly endless, until the "Back to School" banners began appearing in the Sears and Montgomery Ward clothing departments, and we began focusing on a new school year.

Week days were the same, beginning with the morning game shows, the things of which dreams were made. Regular game shows gave away fleets of boats or cavalcades of cars. The shows faded out and the afternoons brought on the matinees. Then by 4:30, Bozo the Clown entertained us, followed by Mayor Art Finley and the renowned spinach king himself, Popeye the Sailor.

Occasionally during the week, I could go with my dad to work. As director of Weights and Measures, he traveled all over the valley visiting businesses, checking the accuracy of scales and other measuring devices. From Napa to Calistoga and all the way to Lake Berryessa, I enjoyed all of the sights and the fascinating points in the Napa Valley where we would visit.

Sometimes the family, when Dad felt the urge, would enjoy weekends at Bodega Bay, tent-camping on the sand dunes of Doran Park Beach. Dad would commercial fish from his fishing trawler he moored in the Bodega Harbor, and we kids would run and play all day on the beach and in the surf.

Then one day, around the second week of August, an invitation addressed to me landed in the mailbox.

"I want to go to Mike Brahman's birthday party," I begged.

"No, I don't think so," Mom said. "I think you spend way too much time with him. I think you should focus your attention on others."

I saw no point in arguing. But luckily, my cousin David had come to visit from Danville, so all wasn't lost.

David was five years old, three years younger than I, but he seemed like the brother that I never had. During his occasional visits, we would hike all over the hills together, play baseball and other sports, or when we were fortunate enough to have a couple of nickels between us, we would visit the Mom and Pop grocery down the road for Sugar Daddies and bubble gum. And of course, we would enjoy our favorite television shows.

One Friday as we sat watching *The Popeye Show*, we both got a wild idea. We should send our names in to KPIX TV and enter the Key Ring Contest.

"Hey, if they pick our names, we could win and get to go on television," I raved.

"Yeah, well, don't get your hopes up," my mother warned. We were determined, nevertheless.

Each day on the show, Mayor Art would have two guests who had won the previous week's Key Ring Contest, one boy and one girl.

In the center of the set sat a huge strongbox, a treasure chest that contained two prizes. Beside the chest sat a board that held six skeleton keys, one of which would unlock the chest. The guests of the day each drew cards or letters with names on them from a huge hopper. Then the two would take turns selecting keys from the rack. Mayor Art would try each key in the lock on the treasure chest. If the key failed, the cards went back into the hopper and the guests would draw two more names. When a chosen key fit the lock, the two lucky entrants, one boy and one girl, would win the prizes in the chest, and had the right to appear on the show one week from that day.

Prizes were the same every day. The girl would receive a Whimsey doll, or, if really lucky, a Tiny Tears doll. The boy would receive a board game, "Melvin the Moon Man," or most often a game called "Notch," a funky little game where the players rolled the dice and moved markers around a board and collected dollar bills called "notches."

But the big prize was the opportunity to be a guest on the program, to meet Mayor Art in person, and to say hello to all of his or her friends.

That Friday we both prepared our names and addresses on envelopes, stamped them, and tucked our entries into the outgoing mail. We couldn't wait until Monday at 5:00 pm when *The Popeye Show* aired on Channel 5.

Monday afternoon, August 24. At five o'clock sharp, David and I were parked in the living room with our glazed eyeballs locked onto the screen of our old black and white TV.

Mayor Art introduced the two guests. They broke for a cartoon. A commercial break. Finally, the next round of the Key Ring Contest began.

Mayor Art gave a hard spin to the huge hopper full of names. The girl guest dipped deep into the hopper and pulled a card.

"We have a girl from Belmont," he announced. The boy drew a name and it turned out to be a boy from Oakland. The girl chose a key from the board.

The key didn't fit. Back to the hopper.

This time the boy chose an envelope.

"We have a young lady from Santa Rosa," Mayor Art called. I still had another chance.

The girl drew.

"And we have young man from St. Helena." Suddenly my heartbeat kicked up a few paces. How many names of boys from St. Helena were in that hopper?

The boy selected a key. Mayor Art slipped the skeleton key into the padlock and twisted it. The key fit.

I sat on the edge of my chair.

"We have a young lady, Jeannette Hart from Santa Rosa, and," he read, reaching for the other envelope, "and a young gentleman, Steven Butler, from St. Helena. Congratulations, you are our winners! You will have the right to be on the show one week from today."

I couldn't believe it. I had won. My feet could not have hit the floor more than two steps as I raced from the living room into the kitchen to tell my mother.

"You what?" she asked, completely dumbfounded. I had won the contest. I would be a guest on the show.

For the next several days, I wandered around in a daze, wondering to myself, how would I feel with every kid from Santa Rosa to San Jose seeing me on TV? How would I see the rest of the world? To whom would I say hello when Mayor Art asked me? And was he really as tall in person as he seemed to be on television? What time would we leave St. Helena in order to be in San Francisco by 5:00 pm for the show? Which way would we go? What about Mom, Dad and my two sisters, Marilyn and Carol? Could they watch too? And David. Would he watch too?

The week crawled.

Finances meant little to me as an eight-year-old. My father worked for the county, so he received his paycheck on the first of each month. That money had to last the entire month. Consequently, we grocery-shopped on the first of the month, and by the end of the month, we were cleaning up the left-overs. The last week of the month was a bad time to plan a trip to the city. My scheduled appearance date was Monday, August 31.

The weekend rolled around. From the feeling I got from my parents, something was definitely amiss.

"We're sorry," my mother went on, "but we're not going to be able to make the trip to the city." She and Dad explained the "end of the month" dilemma.

I was devastated. I couldn't miss this opportunity. Somehow, they would make it happen.

Mom spoke of bridge fares, gasoline, and other expenses. My appearance was doomed.

"We'll make it up to you," Mom promised. "You can go with Dad on Monday when he goes to Lake Berryessa to check stock scales. And afterward, you can go to Mike Brahman's birthday party."

I know I had looked forward to the birthday party. And I always loved the trips out to Lake Berryessa. But they weren't the same. Nevertheless, I knew that this couldn't be any easier for Mom and Dad than it was for me. So I agreed.

Monday the 31st. A dozen or more kids showed up for my friend Mike's party. We shared the usual fare: cake, ice cream, games, and television. In the background I heard the TV broadcasting *The Popeye Show.*

"We regret," I heard Mayor Art speak," that the young man from St. Helena was unable to make it today." I doubt that one single kid at that party realized who that missing boy was. And I wasn't eager to share the secret. Nor was I interested in seeing the show. I spent my time outside playing with other kids.

School started a couple of weeks later, and the Key Ring episode faded into memory. I began the third grade, in which I would meet a whole new school year of challenges. And as time passed, I quickly buried the contest memory deep in a corner of my mind where I would never have to see it or think about it again.

"Nothing worthwhile ever comes easy," warned John Hartmann, my ninth and tenth grade English teacher at Trinity High School.

Years later I think about that summer, of that experience. I wonder to myself: What were the odds that I would win that contest after waiting only one weekend? The girl picked my name. Then the boy chose the right key. People win Lotto jackpots and walk away with millions of dollars on similar odds.

But as I mentioned earlier, I've always believed that the odds had little to do with it. Fate and fortune did. I felt that the Universe was sending me a message. But what was it? Was I receiving validation of my English teacher's words? Most of us get but one magical break like this in a lifetime. These are the breaks that have made many people, at least monetarily, very rich. Mine won me an ill-fated trip to TV Land.

Oh, yes. And a silly board game called "Notch."

Blackberry Jam
by Scotti Butler

Summer 1965: I recall the morning of a sun-drenched summer day in Glen Ellen, California. Warming sunlight came flooding into all the windows, lighting up our tiny rented house. It was one of those summer days when the sun's rays are made visible by the pollen and dust adrift in the breezeless air with the buzz of insects softly assailing one's ears. I knew the blackberries down by the creek would be ready for the picking and was looking forward to canning some for jam.

Urging my son and daughter to finish dressing in shorts and sandals, I began setting out three sizes of buckets for our use. The smallest for three-year-old Lyndel, a cutey with big brown eyes he frequently used to his advantage; the medium-size for six-year-old Pam whose blue eyes sparkled with anticipation to match her smile; and the largest reserved for my use. The children were excitedly bragging to each other about how many berries they would pick, causing me to smile.

Our preparations complete, we hurried down the hill, crossed the narrow country road, and clambered down into the bed of the tiny berry-bush-lined creek. The warm air was redolent with the scent of ripening blackberries and we excitedly commenced picking berries, gradually moving off in three divergent directions.

After nearly an hour of steady picking, we three came together to compare results: My bucket was over half full, Pam's also was over half full. Lyndel displayed one lonely berry in the bottom of his little bucket and, with berry juice making a streak down his chin and belly to the waistband of his shorts, and a woeful expression in his brown eyes, he said, "I tried!"

Later, with the children taking a nap, the rich aroma of simmered blackberries lingeringly permeating the house, and with a deep sense of peace and a job well done, I listened to the "ping" of the canning jars' lids sealing in the yummy jam.

My Name is Legion
By Roger W. Oberbeck

It was a very hot day, 110 degrees Fahrenheit in Suisun City, California with the sun blazing down and heat waves rising off the pavement. Suisun City, on the edge of Suisun Marsh west of the Sacramento River Delta, is the largest brackish water marsh on the west coast, 116,000 acres with many sloughs, ponds and bays. Suisun Marsh is home to the largest population of river otters in the United States.

Joe had been shopping in the new Walmart Superstore on Highway 12 and Walters Road. Joe was leaving through the Garden Center on the west side of the store. Near the exit he noticed the Walmart greeter standing in the hot glaring sun checking the receipts as the customers left the store. He was a big burly, menacing guy with dark-red hair and beard and his skin was a bright angry red as if he had severe sunburn.

When Joe reached him, he noticed that his nametag on his dark-blue Walmart shirt read, *Legion*.

Not wanting to show his unease at the man's appearance, Joe engaged the man in a friendly tone. "How do you like this hot weather?"

The greeter responded in a rough gravelly voice. "I love it; it's just like back home."

"Where's that?"

Legion answered, "Down south...ah...way down south."

Legion's unusual appearance went way beyond simple sunburn; his ears were pointed and his eyes were badly bloodshot. He had two bumps on his head above his forehead, and his teeth were pointed. Joe thought, *This guy has a really bad dentist and he looks kind of scary.* When Joe handed Legion his receipt, Legion marked it with a sharp pointed fingernail and it left a brown mark almost like a burn. Joe felt an irrational fear, like Legion was able to take something valuable from him that he could never reclaim.

Just then another customer came out, with a shopping cart that held five loaves of French bread and two packages of fairly large fish. He was dressed with a long tan robe tied with a rough piece of rope, white undergarment and sandals on his feet. He had tanned skin, long shoulder-length dark-brown hair, and a long tangled dark brown beard down to his chest. He said to the Walmart greeter, in a firm commanding tone, "What is your name?"

The unnerved greeter, responded, "My name is Legion for we are many." His voice was no longer rough and gravely, but raspy and somewhat timid.

Just then a large pack of mangy stray dogs ran past the entrance. Legion begged the robed man, "Send us among the dogs, and allow us to go into them."

The robed man nodded just before the dogs, yipping and howling, ran southeast, across Highway 12 and into the Suisun Marsh. As Joe turned to face the groaning, dazed greeter, who was now leaning against the wall for support, he was astonished to see that the greeter's appearance had completely changed. His skin no longer appeared sunburned, instead it was tanned, his ears weren't pointed, his eyes were no longer bloodshot, the bumps on his head were gone. His teeth were no longer pointed, and his nametag now read, *Legend.*

Joe watched as the robed man walked out into the parking lot to a group of about twelve men dressed in similar garb.

One of them called out, "There you are, Rabbi, we thought you had left us."

Rabbi replied, "It is not my time to leave, yet."

Aha, it's a religious cult, but that robed man seems strangely familiar; for some reason I have an urge to follow him. I feel that I can learn something important from him. Curiosity and logic raged war in Joe's mind with each involuntary step he took toward the robed man.

I Stand on the Shoulders

By Grant Perryman

I stand on the shoulders
Of those who have come before me.
I am the present looking to the past
A connection, a link, to all that was before me.

I stand on the shoulders
Of those who have come before me.
Those that gave me life, provided me with food,
    love and warmth.
Through tragedy and invasion, conquest and
    occupation.
Surviving slavery and genocide, racism and J.C.
    apartheid.
They gave all they had and when they had
    nothing else to give
They gave their all—that I might live.
They remained strong...so...
I could stand on their shoulders.

I stand on the shoulders
Of those who have come before me.
My inheritance is boundless and unique.
I am a diagram of cultures, a poem of traditions.
I am a sacred story woven in the past and
　　threaded for the present.
Hallowed ingredients, seasoned by time, recipes of
　　wisdom that gently guide.
I am a historical collection, an archive of old, a
　　library of knowledge quick to listen,
I hear, I repeat the words that carried me here...so
　　I understand how
I could stand on their shoulders.

I stand on the shoulders
Of those who have come before me.
I stand humbly and respectfully, no foolish
　　arrogance or pride.
I stand here today because of my ancestors who
　　lived, fought and died.
The breath they gave me, the heart that beats
　　within me cannot disrespect the life they
bequeathed me.
I have to live my life with honor and not
　　disdain, as a tribute for all their sacrifice
　　and pain...so...
I can stand straight and tall on their shoulders.

I stand on the shoulders
Of those who have come before me.
Even today so many obstacles are trying to
    overtake me,
Violence and hatred, drugs and alcohol, crime and
    unemployment.
Injustices surround me, unfairness plagues me
    and like an evil injection,
They pierce my mind, contaminate my spirit, and
    infect my heart with anger and malice.
But I can't feel sorry for myself, I can't stay down,
    I can't allow rage to decimate my soul
I have to stand up, I have to do what is right, I
    have to fight this deadly vice
I have to go on, I have to find a way, I have to be
    strong, for soon one day
Someone will have to stand on my shoulders.

Epilogue
I am the sum total of all my ancestors
A map, a quilt, a tablecloth of poetry
I unravel the threads to discover my heritage
African Native and European filigree

I am the strongest of the strong, the bravest
    of the brave
I am nature's mightiest breed
I have a duty, I have a responsibility, I have a good
    debt to repay
I strive for education, I give back to community

Southern Sugar
by Naomi Connor

The streetcar bell was audible in the distance. Clear blue skies and laughter were abundant. The French Quarter, charismatic as it always is, beckoned me at a chance for adventure. Surely, adventure awaits. Such southern charm and hospitality is true fortune. Genuine charm is the epitome of wealth and the currency of the south.

Strolling down the cobblestone street, the warm, favorable New Orleans atmosphere intensified the experience. I amused myself with the many local performers, restaurants and street vendors. The antique, decorative glass and mystique shops tickled my brain with images of the stories and tales of life in the Big Easy. Entering the structures was akin to visiting family. It was familiar. Conversation was easy with a sprinkle of history and a splash of laughter along with a token purchased to stash away in my already overstuffed luggage. Feelings of generosity abound.

New Orleans is the hub of southern hospitality. Genuine warmth oozes from smiles and salutations. The intrigue and culture of the area opens doors to the imagination. Stepping into the stores that boast mystical legends and myths associated with New Orleans are as stimulating as the buildup to finding the culprit in a fictional who-dun-it! Melodious sounds and southern comfort is New Orleans' trademark. New Orleans welcomes you!

New Orleans' residents, especially the mature ones, are reared in the art of hospitality. There she stood, tall, slender, sculptured, with engraved facial creases consistent with that of a smoker. She was poised with a cigarette between her second and third fingers, taking a gentle draw and exhaling in time to greet me with a nod and a greeting that has since been so dear to me.

"Hello, sugar."

Those two words; sweet, elegant, and endearing. This southern colloquialism could not be mistaken for anything other than what it is. Precious. Her restaurant attire; white shirt and black pants was reminiscent of old black and white movies. My thoughts dictated that Grandma should be home with her grand kids. She should be home relaxing and enjoying life.

Who was I to think that she wasn't enjoying her life? Her gentleness, the inner joy that she transferred, unmasked this true heart of the person standing before me. My stomach churned at conflicting thoughts. The starched, white and black attire took me again to the images portrayed in black and white movies, but now the scene was that of servitude. I was in the south. This revelation cast a repressive shadow over my joy.

My journey continued. It wasn't long before I'd realized that I was hungry. Reading the menus that were conveniently displayed in restaurant windows were as welcomed as the seduction of the many aromas of sweets and spices that filled the air. I struggled with my decision, but I would make it a priority to visit as many of these venues as possible before my departure. I decided on jambalaya, salad, French bread and bread pudding with rum sauce. Ice cold sweet tea with the meal goes without saying. It's the south where sweet tea is a staple. I was equally delighted with the century old building that offered this gathering of strangers, young and old, to enjoy their meal. What is it about this place that makes the everyday, fresh-baked tube of French bread a soft, crunchy delicacy? What is it about an everyday coffee spot that provides world-class entertainment as one sips on coffee and nibbles on beignets that makes it such an inexplicable experience? Southern hospitality at its best!

Taking me back to the grandmotherly figure acknowledging me on the crowded streets of New Orleans, the aromatic winds of deliciousness, the rhythm of kids tap-dancing in the streets with sellers of pralines on various street corners and the sweet blend of gardenia and magnolia blossoms that are rampant in the city; southern sweetness is prevalent. The streets are controlled chaos.

Happiness and joy came to life as sweet, southern hospitality. In contradiction, the laid-back calm of the day gave "sugar" the embodiment of southern sweetness. Being greeted as "sugar" is as warm as a hug in winter and as endearing as a mother's kiss.

Remembering the sugar matron is a calming respite from life's emotional overload. Her whereabouts and activities since Hurricane Katrina give me pause. My wishes are that she is safe and enjoying her grandchildren, making pralines and with her sweet, southern charm, greeting everyone that she meets by calling them "sugar."

The Sounds of Love

By Janell Michael

I knew I was created for love. From the first note to the very last, it was my purpose to bring love to the people around me. Love is a language I speak well. I never imagined I would go on such a journey to find my ultimate place of love!

It all started in a piano factory in Baltimore, Maryland. I come from a long line of handmade pianos created by Wilhelm Knabe. He began the company in 1835. Their work was known for its high standards and beautiful finishes. Each Knabe has a personality of its own. The very soul of the instrument can be felt in its rich tones.

Many famous people over the years either owned or played a Knabe piano. Of course, my brothers came in different sizes and styles from me. I am just a humble upright myself. Francis Scott Key ordered a custom-built square grand piano for his home. Tchaikovsky, the great composer, played one of my grand piano brothers at the opening of Carnegie

Hall in 1891. In 1926 another of my brothers was chosen as the official grand piano of the New York Metropolitan Opera.

At Graceland, Elvis Presley owned a Knabe grand piano. It was refinished in white with gold trim just as the king wished. This Knabe brother had a wonderful history of being played in the 1930's by Duke Ellington, Count Basie and Cab Callaway at the Ellis Auditorium in Memphis, Tennessee before it came to his home with Elvis. But as happens with so many of my brothers, a new piano was purchased and this beautiful Knabe was taken off to storage.

Of course, my journey as an upright piano was not as "grand" as my piano brothers. Forgive the pun. But, nonetheless, I have a history of my own. For me it all started when I was purchased by a nightclub owner building his business on Bourbon Street in New Orleans. His idea was to open a modern day "Speak-easy" with a dash of burlesque thrown in. My job was to be the background voice to carry all the other performers.

Many of the songs they played on me spoke of love. In my heart I knew this was not the kind of love I was destined to play. I stayed there for more years than I'd like to count. Song after song, I kept hoping I would hear the true love I was meant to play. It never came.

What did come was a terrible flood. The rain came in sheets. The wind was the loudest sound I had ever heard as it raced by the building. Suddenly, my stage was surrounded by dirty, smelly water. I was on an island I thought I would never get off of.

After months, which felt like years, the water began to recede. I was finally moved to a warehouse for safekeeping.

It was at this warehouse that I met Joe. He was the night watchman. Late every night, Joe would seek me out. His touch was gentle. The songs he played were hopelessly sad. He called it the Blues. I wanted so much to cheer him up. He just seemed to be stuck in the midst of sadness and woe.

I was so happy the day a young family came to buy me. The mother sat down and played a lovely melody that was new to me. The children clapped and cheered as their father said they could bring the piano home as long as they all kept up on their lessons to become as good a pianist as their mother. I was so happy to be out of that dark sad warehouse. I wondered what Joe was going to do to pass the night without me.

Kyle, Skyler and Hudson all faithfully spent thirty minutes each day practicing the scales and chords their teacher requested of them. I sat through endless rounds of "Chop Sticks" and elementary versions of "Ode to Joy". My ears rang with each missed note and final arpeggio played as they relinquished their spot on the bench to the next sibling.

In time, I did see some improvement, especially from Skyler. She must have gotten her musical genes from her mother. Skyler even began writing songs. I was thrilled with her use of words and harmony to form a different kind of love song. Not like what I heard in New Orleans or even the blue songs played by Joe. There was hope in her songs.

Eventually, Kyle and Hudson stopped playing me all together. They were too busy with sports and girls. Skyler also stopped playing me since she was leaving for college. The mother dusted me weekly and once in a while sat down to play a number or too. Mostly I was just another piece of furniture with no notes of love to share. The final blow came when the dad lost his job. He and his wife needed to "downsize", whatever that meant. The next thing I knew, I was sitting in a Thrift store cluttered with other castoffs. I was covered with so many doilies, vases and figurines no one could play me at all. What had life come to? How was I ever going to find my place of love?

That's when Pastor Joel walked into the store; his every stride carrying great purpose. He needed a piano for the rescue mission down the street. He came and looked me over from top to bottom. I knew my soundboard was solid and I still had all my ivory keys. Joel asked the owner if he could remove all the bric-a-brac from the top of me. The owner helped and together I was free again.

As Pastor Joel opened me up and sat down to play, I learned of a new way to be set free. I was over-whelmed by what I heard. Could it be? Had I finally found my place of love? He began with "Amazing Grace, how sweet the sound that saved a wretch like me" and finished with "Just as I am, without one plea but that Thy blood was shed for me." Every person stopped and listened as we continued our little concert. They all clapped as Pastor Joel finished. I couldn't have been more proud! The owner wiped away a tear and told the chaplain he could have the piano for no charge. They shook hands with smiles all around. Later that day a group of men in various forms of dress and stature came to move me to my new home. They didn't have far to go as they pushed me down the street.

That was many years ago. I have never been happier. Every day someone comes and plays the most beautiful songs of love on my welcoming keys. I have finally found the love I was destined to be part of. Jesus was the key all along. I am so thankful that in my small way, I help others find that same love. My destiny with love was all found in Jesus.

Spiritual Beats
By Eddrick Jerome

West African Coastal Region, 1838

The village elders summoned Sunsesi the Conjurer to
the small hut. They needed his magic to cast the bad
spirit, Shongira, known for uninhibited debauchery,
out of Malwewa. Malwewa allowed her lust for Idris,
not her husband, to subdue her, and commit an act
of delicious foolishness. Her husband threatened
to stone her until the elders stepped in. She was
only sixteen.

Sunsesi brought his goatskin bag which was
filled with powders and foul-smelling herbs. He also
brought pieces of flint, water, a drum, and the bones
of a small calf. At his urging, Malwewa lay down
on the dirt floor. The midday sun burst in through
large cracks in the mud hut. Sunsesi wasn't sure
that his conjuring would work. The elders looked
at him with concerned grimaces, which said, "This
better work."

Sunsesi called upon the calming spirit, Jolnmphe, to arrive and talk to the bones of the calf. His call lasted more than an hour before he felt signs of Jolnmphe's presence. The air turned cool and the sunlight disappeared, leaving the hut in gray darkness. Sunsesi struck the pieces of flint and lit the dry foul-smelling herbs. Smoke filled the hut. Some of the elders coughed before feeling the euphoric effects of the herb smoke. All the while Malwewa lay in stillness. The only movement from her was the sweat trickling down her neck.

Sunsesi called out to Jolnmphe at the top of his lungs. His screams frightened Malwewa. But there, in the herb-smoked light, appeared a little shadow on the east side of the hut. The flames caused the shadow to move with life. Sunsesi stopped calling and appeared surprised at this development. The bones rattled. Sunsesi cried out again.

"Spirit of Jolnmphe, we are humbled in your presence! Shongira has tormented our village! This child bride is worthy of saving! If the elders say she is cured her husband must not kill her! They call upon you to cast out Shongira!" He began playing a polyrhythmic pattern on the drums. Some of the backbones of the elders instinctively moved in time with the beat.

Malwewa growled and spat a glob of spit onto the floor. Sunsesi doused the herbs with the water to put the flames out. The smoke intensified and the elders nodded in approval. He began to play the drum again. At that moment the door of the hut flew open and little Ikibo, six and cute, entered with wild-eyed curiosity. The drumbeat lured him to the hut. One of the elders scolded him and escorted him out by the ear. But the beat lingered in his head.

Atlantic Ocean, 1858

The slave ship rocked back and forth making a ghastly wheeze. Ikibo, weak from hunger and thirst, drifted in and out of consciousness. His reality was forever degraded yet the beat lingered in his head.

Danville, Virginia, 1878

Ikibo used courage and guile to conduct his church services. Music was the foundation of his ministry because he couldn't read the bible he carried. Voice, rhythmic clapping, and drumming carried the daylong Sunday services. Every song, fast or slow, had some semblance of the beat he knew from his childhood. Unbeknownst to him, the beat made some of the women feel things that conflicted with his teaching. Sensual urges gripped willful loins during the songs. Ikibo didn't know that the beat conjured up Shongira, and drove the women crazy with lust.

Hampton University, Hampton, Virginia, 1908

Jester Jackson played the drums like few students could. He'd turned the slow methodical patterns he'd learned in class into syncopated bursts that lifted the Hampton University students to their feet in orgiastic dancing. Jester used his skillful rhythm patterns to speak to the crowd. His drumming was so intoxicating that it got him kicked out of school for "moral turpitude". But that was a lucky break for Jester because John Wilkerson, protégé of Scott Joplin, heard his playing and invited him to join a ragtime band he was forming. Jester played on instinct and relied on the patterns his grandfather "Icky Bo" had taught him many years ago. Within six months Wilkerson's band was the talk of New York City.

Harlem, New York, 1938

Jester Jackson Jr. "The Rhythmic Wonder" was known for standing up on the high hat. A master of the two and four, Jester Jr. was in high demand for his drumming skills and acrobatic showman-ship. Duke Ellington recruited him. Bix Biederbecke wanted him for a swing band he was forming. But Jester was happy playin' in the house band at Smalls Paradise, Harlem's most notorious club. Jester Jr. played with a wildness that drove the women crazy. And he never went home alone.

Augusta, Georgia, 1968

Jonas Jackson, son of Jester Jr., played drums for a short time with James Brown during a transformative period that reshaped popular music. Their collaboration, though not well-documented, produced some interesting new ways for the drums to be featured at the forefront of songs. James and Jonas created "the one", a new pattern based in large part on something that Jonas used to warm up with before he played. James loved it and he'd dance energetically whenever he heard it. Jonas always liked to tell James, "My daddy told me that this beat is very powerful and is a surefire way to get them panties." The spirit of Shongira was now immersed in every jukebox, record store, and radio station in the United States. The listeners had no idea that the "funky drumming" on James' songs was actually calls to summon Shongira. As James was apt to say, "Get up! I feel like a sex machine!"

Cleveland, Ohio, 1988

J Jack, popular rapper, had the hit of the summer of '88. His song, "Pump it Hard and Pump it Fast" was played on every radio station. Millions of copies were sold and kids were doing the Pump It dance all over the world. His producer used a snippet of an old James Brown song and the beat was infectious. J Jack's grandfather, Jester Jr., recognized the beat, and told his friends at the convalescence home, "My grandson's music is goin' to get some girl pregnant."

University of California at Berkeley, 2018

Dr. Curtis Peters, renowned African-American music scholar and cultural critic, approached the microphone at the lecture hall which was filled to capacity with students, artists and journalists from around the world. His highly popular book, *Spiritual Beats – The Subliminal Affects of the Bass and Drum*, sent shockwaves through the hip-hop community and created an inferno of debate on all social media platforms. He began to speak:

"Let me begin my remarks with this warning. The hip-hop music of today, with its reliance on low frequency beat patterns and poly-rhythmic drumming, is filling our world with subliminal messages rooted in the archeological past of ancient West African spiritual rituals. The beats of today harken back to a time in African culture when drums were the way to speak directly with the spiritual world. My research has conclusively proven that many of the beats that permeate hip-hop are conjuring in nature and communicate with thousands of trickster spirits of the ethereal realm.

Some will argue that hip-hop beats are at the forefront of crime, violence, and wanton sex in our youth culture. While that may be a subject for further debate, my research has shown that particular beats call out to spirits of lust, spirits of treachery, and many more to spirits of death. This, and the overall impact of sub optimal social environments, has affected our young people in a traumatic way. The beats have a subconscious physical and mental affect on the behavior of young women and young men. They are blind to the real messages that the beats convey and they succumb to the subliminal pleasures and pressures that inhabit their bodies and minds. Thank you for coming out today and I will now take your questions..."

Louise & Alice
A Life-Changing Friendship
By Ruth LaMell

Today I take a trip down memory lane. I often visit there lately. I am beginning to think that this could be attributed to the approaching of my golden years, and all the losses that I have suffered in my life.

I am now reflecting on my high school days in my hometown of Abbeville, Louisiana in the early sixties. The schools in Vermilion Parish had just begun to integrate, and we as Black Americans, having had the comforts of our own schools and teachers, were anxious about all of this. However, the change did occur.

I am reminded of one student with whom I became friends during this great transition. My name is Louise. My friend's name is Alice. I am African American, and Alice is Anglo- Saxon. We met in an English class in nineteen sixty-four. At that time racial tension was brewing at boiling point. Black

Americans were fighting for civil rights, and not taking "NO" for an answer.

This day in my new school, this white girl swooshed past me, all dressed up in designer clothing: shoes, purse, the whole nine yards. She sat in front of me and turned to me and said, "Hi, my name is Alice." This is how our friendship started.

I often wondered why she wanted to become my friend. She seemingly had it all. Her father was a dentist, her mother worked at the local school board as an administrator, and she lived in a gated community, wearing the finest of clothes, and driving the year's latest super sports car. My life and background were totally different. I lived in the ghetto, wore clothing from the thrift shops, or what my mother who was a domestic could sew for me, and I took the bus to school. Nevertheless, I had a good family structure: a loving mother and father who worked the cane fields, and two beautiful sisters. I made good grades in school and knew that I would eventually make something of my life as an educator.

Alice and I connected well, however, the unspoken was that we knew that our friendship had a border wall between it. We could only go so far. I would never be invited to her house, and neither she to mine. Nevertheless, our friendship endured. She was very curious about Black History, and I became her teacher. She had a great interest in the African-American poet Maya Angelou.

There were times in our relationship that Alice was subdued and sad. I could smell alcohol on her breath, even though she tried to hide this with a mouthful of mints. Whenever I asked her questions regarding her feelings and actions, she never explained to me any of what she was feeling at the time.

We graduated from high school, Alice went her way, and I prepared to enroll in USL (University of Louisiana at Lafayette) twenty-one miles away from my hometown. I had studied very hard and was granted a four-year scholarship to USL. During that time, I found out that Alice had moved away without trying to contact me and say goodbye.

Upon my graduation from college with my B.A. in education, I was employed as a teacher with the state department working with underprivileged students, helping them to grow, and become responsible members of the communities in which they lived.

One day I picked up the local newspaper and saw that Alice had married one of our Louisiana State Assemblymen, and was living in the city of New Orleans, Louisiana. I felt joy; I wanted happiness for her and prayed that she had found it. The years went by and my work eventually took me to New Orleans. Upon arriving in New Orleans, I checked into the Holiday Inn Hotel. As I unpacked my luggage, I became aware that I had forgotten to pack certain toiletries items. The hotel's gift shop was on the first floor and I went down to purchase my missing items.

Upon entering, I noticed a seemingly familiar face. I told myself, "This cannot be her: eyes puckered, waistline thickened. However, I knew that it was her." We looked directly into each other's faces, and the room became filled with laughter and tears. I had found my old friend Alice, and it had taken me fifteen years. The feeling was almost kindred, even though we were not related.

I could sense that she wanted to talk to me in privacy, therefore, I invited her up to my room. She proceeded to tell me that she always wanted to be like me: competent, self-assured, and confident about what I wanted out of life. I began to envision what she had gone through all these years. Alcoholism and drug abuse had become her way out, gradually taking its toll on her beauty. I was able to understand that she had never been as happy as I thought, with all the material things that were imposed upon her. Her marriage to an older man was only to protect her from her fears, even though she eventually fell in love with him. She had two beautiful daughters and a loving husband. Nevertheless, she needed more. I sensed my friend needed a purpose. She needed something that she could feel good about.

I introduced her to my life's work and found out that she was very interested. I recommended that she talk to her husband about introducing a bill that would implement funds for the underprivileged in low income neighborhoods, providing scholarships for academic achievements.

I think about her great epiphany: going back to school, becoming a state assemblywoman, helping and promoting great programs for the underprivileged. I look back with contentment, feeling blessed to have met my friend Alice in that hotel gift shop on that day. The day that changed both of our lives for the better.

Time and circumstances have a way of connecting long lost relationships: lost loves, friendships and feelings. One must never think that the pursuit of materialism will bring about great joy and lasting contentment. There are prerequisites to all of this. One must feel good about themselves, to inherit the joy and contentment that is associated with wealth and materialism.

On the other hand, they who believe in themselves can live lives of quiet contentment, without the desire of great possessions. This wealth resides in knowing themselves; freeing them to expose themselves into great works. For these individuals, if wealth should enter their paths, they are not changed by its weight; they can handle the weight, moving into the direction of their life's mission.

This is what I discovered regarding my and Alice's rekindled friendship. I also discovered that when we step out of ourselves in an unselfish way to help others, we usually end up finding our true self.

Visitor
By Carl Weber

We are here only to visit,
With our portion of allotted time.
Eyes recording each experience,
And sometimes to cry,
When we are overwhelmed.

Coming to realize: not to own too much,
Not to hold too tight, not to call Earth home.
The flowing out of hand,
The naked in and naked out of this world.

We are but borrowers of this planet,
Renting attitudes sometimes too serious,
Screaming and demanding too much,
And paying with arthritic hands.

Only to arrive at a longing to leave:
Disappointed at sights seen,
Eyes overwhelmed again,
Wishing for the unseen.
Living to learn much. Then just to leave.
And leaving the earth with nothing.
We learn to let go of the things of the Earth.
And move on. Move on. Move on.

Test Games
By Patricia Vincent

I see this is all a test.
You like to play little test games with me.
No! I'm no pushover.
Not to be looked over,
See the games that you play
To get in my head is now over.

You no longer can have the control
That I let you once have
Over my mind, body, and soul.
See cause the test you're trying to run is old.
Truth be told when it comes to these tests
I'm the best.

Bet I can ace them all
And come with a new test
To teach you a thing or two
I'm the best at reading, adding, subtracting,
and solving problems.

So when you want to run these tests and
    play these mind games
Bring your "A" game
Because there will be nothing less.
My mind, body, and soul are not a test
So don›t test me,
Game over.

The Promise
By Carole Morrison

Talk about a long drink of water. Over six-feet tall and maybe ninety-five pounds after being caught in a downpour, ruddy cheeks, and a smile wider than God intended for such a narrow face, and you have Columbus Moore.

Columbus could have been somewhere between eighty and a hundred years old when I met him as a twenty-year-old living in Los Angeles. Columbus lived across the street from me with his wife, Nannie. They were both transplants from the cotton fields of West Texas, blown to California decades back by the Dust Bowl.

Columbus found himself a good job with the city, bought a little home and paid it out. He and Nannie raised three good girls there.

As Columbus likes to tell it, when he settled on Nannie for his bride, he took out to the cotton fields to ask her daddy's permission even though he was a grown man of twenty-five, and Nannie was a grown woman of twenty-three. "That's how country folks were expected to do," he said.

"Young fella, I'm tellin' you, you're marrin' a doctor bill," warned the daddy. "That gal has been a sickly one since the day she was borned," he went on, stooped over, both raw hands grabbing at bolls and stuffing cotton into the long sack trailing him, never stopping to look up.

"Well, I reckon I can pay the doctor bills the same as you," Columbus offered. And that was that. Columbus and Nannie found them a preacher man coming across the street and got him to recite their vows with them right there on the sidewalk in front of the courthouse.

Sixty-five years have passed since that day in the cotton fields of Big Spring, Texas where Nannie's daddy more or less said Columbus could marry his daughter.

Nannie did stay sickly just like her daddy said she would, ailing from one thing then another, and with birthing three babies, and finally with the cancer that took her. Columbus paid for it all. Just like he promised her daddy he would if he could have Nannie for his wife.

Bless his heart.

Mother, Her Story — My View
By Nina Pringle

"Mother" Pauline E. Parchman was born July 27, 1934. She was the youngest of eight children. Her father died of pneumonia complications when she was an infant, eight months old. She was raised on a farm where she had to work very hard and only had an eighth-grade education. Mother's mother, my grandmother, whom I didn't get to know very well, Willie Easley, did very well for herself in the south even without a husband. She raised her eight children on a farm with various kinds of animals and gardens, owning the land and her home. Mother was raised in a very strict environment and sought to leave home at an early age; by then Mother had learned significant values that she would use in life.

Mother was beautiful and shapely in her younger years and had no trouble finding a husband. She was fifteen years old when she married a much older man, and sixteen years old when she had her first child. By 1968, Mother had ten children—six boys and four girls. Mother packed up her ten children and moved across country from the small city of Erin, Tennessee to the big city of Oakland, California. Mother made the best decision of her life when she moved to California. She gave her children a better chance at life and a better education by bringing them out of the south and gave them an opportunity to escape the prejudices that she herself had to endure.

Mother moved into an all-white neighborhood in 1968 with ten black children. As she became friends with the only white lady that would befriend her at that time, she was told that the neighbors feared her being there and with ten black children. They thought her children would destroy the neighborhood. As time passed some of the white neighbors moved away. Mother was told by the ones who stayed that her ten children were the best-behaved children in the neighborhood. Mother didn't allow her children to run free or to bother the neighbors. She bought a house large enough for her ten children with a big backyard so that they didn't have to play in the streets or in the neighbors' yards. Ironically, once the other neighbors started to befriend Mother they would complain to her about the white lady's two boys that first befriended her.

After moving to California and marrying her second husband, Mother had two more boys, giving her eight boys and four girls. While Mother raised her twelve children she also took part in raising some of the neighborhood children and her children's friends. With twelve children you can imagine that one of us always had a friend over especially since we weren't allowed to go to other people's houses. Our friends had to come to our home. By the time anyone left our home they had been fed, made to feel at home, and scolded if need be, thus, the reason for everyone calling her, "Mother." As far back as I can remember she has been referred to as Mother by all of our friends. Though our friends are all grown up now they still come to visit and still refer to her affectionately as Mother.

We are all grown now and living in California and gather at Mother's house nearly every holiday to catch up with each other and to celebrate. Most of us have raised our children by her example. Seven of her children live very close to her in the city and her youngest daughter lives with her to help care for her and her second husband, who is ninety-six years old.

Mother, whom I love dearly and am very proud of for raising her twelve children and several grand-children, with a strong hand, I might add, is now eighty-four years old. Mother also became a foster parent for many years after her own children were grown. I have tremendous respect for her because I am a foster parent and have been for the past sixteen years. I have seen mothers with only one child fail at being a mother. I have seen and cared for children who have been abused and neglected for various rea-sons. So, I recognize the blessings of my childhood having come from a family of twelve children.

Mother never abused nor neglected us, thank God. It could have been a horrible life trying to raise twelve children, but Mother loved her children and refused to let us do without. Mother, of course, could not give us everything in life that we desired during our childhood, as even the greatest parent can't do. But I thank God that we had everything that we needed. I look back now and understand that there are so many different reasons that I or any of my siblings could be given as to why our lives went the way it did or why we were raised the way that we were raised. Watching Mother and having been raised by her has made me want to be the best parent that I can be.

I only have three children and it wasn't easy raising them even with my husband being present and hands on. After my third child I knew that I had had enough and didn't want any more children. I don't know how Mother did it, and still does it. She always has one or two children in her house whenever I go to visit. My siblings and I are always telling her that she doesn't need to still take care of children at her age, but she doesn't listen. I suppose they help keep her active and useful. I can understand how she feels though, from experience, being a mother: the love that you have inside and the joy that you feel when you see the smile on a child's face; when you know that you have made them happy or to feel loved, it is a precious life experience for a woman.

The love from a mother and the love of being a mother is an experience that every woman should have the privilege of experiencing. Being a mother does not come with a guidebook. We are lucky if we had a good example, but even then it is a whole new experience when you birth your own child. We do what we know how to do with what we have been given in life. I feel so blessed to have had the mother that I had.

I am not suggesting that we had the perfect childhood, on the contrary. I believe that God has a plan for all of us and that we have to go through certain things with certain people to mold us into the person or people that God wants us to be. I love my life as it is right now and I know that I had to come through all of the disappointments in life to get to where I am now. I appreciate so much the upbringing that I had and the siblings that I was raised with. I hope that they have gotten to a place in their hearts and minds to feel the same way.

I know it is difficult for most people to forgive or to get over things that may or may not have happened in their lives and to move forward in life with no regrets. Knowing God has made it easy for me to take my past experiences and see them as a blessing for my future. For example, being the fifth child of twelve and a girl, I felt that I was the Cinderella of my family. I had to babysit my younger siblings and I had to cook and clean while my older siblings were allowed to go out with their friends. Of course, I hated it at the time, but now, as I look back, I have come to appreciate that I was put in that position. It made me a good mother and wife. Mother was strict, overprotective, and sheltered us, especially the girls. She made sure that we respected ourselves and that we did not put ourselves in any position with men that would get us into trouble or abused.

From the time that I was of age to remember, I never saw a hungry day. I always had a roof over my head. I always had a warm bed to sleep in at night. What I thank God for most, is that I always had my mother. Even though sometimes it was a struggle, she never gave up or threw in the towel. I would be very selfish to not appreciate that. I hope that all of my siblings agree with me and appreciate our mother for who she is and for the struggles that she may have had in raising us. Whatever I thought I lacked in my childhood, or whatever I may have gone through is nothing compared to what children endure today.

Love your mother. Honor and respect your mother no matter what kind of life you had, or think you should have had. She is your mother and you will never be able to replace her with anyone else; she is the one that God gave you. Please, understand that the decisions that mothers make at the time they make them are what they understand at the time to be the best decision for you. It doesn't always turn out right or end up being the best decision, but it is all that they have at the time and what they think is best for you at that time. It is up to you to find the blessing and the love in whatever life she gave you. She is the one that gave you life and that in itself is enough. You are here. What you make of your life now is your decision, not hers.

Take what you feel was lacking in your life or relationship with your mother and make a better future out of it for yourself and for your children. We can't hate our mothers because they failed to give us what we needed out of life or because we needed more from them. God gave us the mothers and families that we have and we can question him all day as to why, but we may never get an answer. It is what we do with it once we become of age that counts. If you are grown and are still holding a grudge or harboring ill feelings against your mother for some lack in your childhood, I urge you to let it go and love your mother unconditionally while she is still here for you to do so. If you don't, it will continue to control your life and your relationship with your mother and that would be a shame.

If your mother is gone, forgive her and know that she did what she knew to do at the time with what she had to do it with. It may help to put yourself in her position, her life, with her education, circumstances, abuses, etc. You may not know what your mother may have suffered to make her the person that she is or was to cause her to raise you the way she did. Mothers don't tell you of all the abuses they suffered themselves in life. They suffer through it in silence while trying to raise you. I believe that most mothers do the best that they can though it still may not be enough, they try.

I think about Mother leaving here all the time now. I try to prepare my mind for the loss of her, but I don't know how I am going to feel or what I am going to do when that awful day comes. I hope you know that I appreciate you, Mother, and the life that you created for me and so many others. After reading this, I hope that my own children understand my position as a mother and the decisions that I have made regarding their lives. I hope that what I have said will inspire everyone to love and appreciate their mother a little more before you have to express it at her memorial service when it is too late for her to enjoy it and reciprocate.

I want you to know, Mother, that I love you with all of my heart and whenever you leave me I will miss you terribly. I will now wear my middle name proudly. My name is Nina Pauline Pringle. For all of my life I have been embarrassed to tell anyone what my middle name is because it seems and sounds so old-fashioned. But now that I understand who this woman is that bears this name and the struggle that she must have had raising twelve children, I am proud to be her namesake.

In honor of my mother, I hope mothers reading this will have the courage to use her story as a tool to better themselves as a mother or even a person. Mother never drank, never did drugs, she didn't even smoke. She is strong and healthy for her age and we hope to have her with us for a very long time. The half has not been told of Mother's eighty-four years, two husbands, twelve children, and upbringing in the south. God bless you, Mother, and mothers all over the world. I hope to tell your whole story one day.

S – H – E

By Tony Lorenzo Bess

S-H-E. Her true self is revealed simply in the spelling.

S tells us that she's sexy, stubborn, sensitive, and smart.
H says she's, helpful, humble, heartwarming, and honest.
E expresses that she is essential, extraordinary, emotional, and educated.

She is the one we call Queen, Princess, Sweetheart, Honey, and Babe.
A leader, a poet, a musician, an entrepreneur, a pilot, an astronaut, a soldier. A chef, an actress, an inventor, a planner, a designer, an author, a director, and a minister. She is my reason for being, the reason for my existence. I give her credit for my purpose. Representative of someone's mother, another's lover, in someone's song, she is desire, and to be desired. Envy can make her ugly to some, yet her beauty is a blessing to many. She is loved and honored, but can be hated too.

She is the music of our world. Songs about her say, "Her fire is desire." Her rhythm goes with the blues. Her rock goes with a roll. She gives only a glimpse of her soul. Singing songs of triumph and failure, respect and disrespect, love that is gained and sometimes lost. The melody of her sensual voice puts a baby to sleep and makes a grown man cry. Some call her, "The Greatest Love of All". Others just see her and say, "Oh my, my, my!"

Captured in movies, she's fast and furious. An amazing, wonderful, and glorious star! On the screen and in the scene she is a woman's idol and a man's dream! Lady in Red, Pretty Woman, Mary Poppins, lady sings the blues, the girlfriend next door, the wife living that ordinary life. The daughter, the friend; her story never ends.

Her beauty brightens the sky, even the stars can't lie! Her scent is in the wind and with every breath, you take a part of her in. She is all God made her to be. The one and only, S-H-E!

Another Chance

By Kelley Marable

In my fifty-three years, almost as soon as I lie down for bed I fall asleep in a matter of minutes. I never had any trouble falling fast asleep. But for most of my life almost every night around 3 a.m. my eyes open on their own and my mind actively starts sorting out my life, my goals, my mistakes, my decisions, my family, my successes and so on, and no matter what I can't stop it. What is something trying to tell me?

So, I think, cry, pray, give thanks, regret, and question, but I never stop believing that if I give the best of me and keep trying to do good, good will come to me. However, it never stops there. I am often asking questions. Did I accomplish any goals? Why were my young years turbulent? Why did my first child die before the age of 3? What would she be like now? Why do people continually lie to me so much? Why is it hard for me to say no? Why did they cheat on me? Why didn't I stand up for myself? Why do I often feel forgotten about? When will I retire? When am I going to travel to other countries? When am I going to win the lottery? Why didn't I have parents dedicated to me? What is my role? What more can I do to be a better person, friend, wife, mother? Do my kids really know how much I love them? What am I cooking for dinner tomorrow? Then I turn over look at the clock and my stress rises because I have been up thirty minutes too long. Not only does my total being ignore this, but my mind keeps going. As I sort out how my day is going to go, I continue by pondering my future and its possibilities. I finally say a prayer, get snuggled in and fall asleep for a short while, only to wake up tired and wanting a few more minutes, fifty-five would be great!

I listen to a motivational speaker as I get ready for my day. Making sure my clothes, hair, jewelry, and everything else, especially my smile, are just right. No one will ever know by looking at about my sleepless nights, losses, heart break, unfulfilled dreams, disappointments, sadness, or tears I cried. I emulate triumph, hope, encouragement, thankfulness, faithfulness, love, fairness, and positivity. My ultimate desire is for positivity. I seek throughout my day to accomplish as much as I can to make a difference to anyone who will be in my presence for any amount of time no matter their age, background, status, gender, financial or emotional state. I have come to realize most people have gone through something that has taken a deep part of their soul away leaving an empty space inside. And if my doing something simple gives them just a little spark of joy, and helps them see clearer maybe just maybe they will choose to become a positive difference in the life of someone else today Thoughts like motivates me.

After what I have in endured in my life it would be easy for me to be selfish, judgmental, bitter and hard. But throughout my life The Almighty Creator of this great Universe has allowed me to witness indescribable and undeniable works of kindness, mercy, grace and good karma.

At the end of the day when I finally settle into bed and effortlessly fall asleep, again I wake up at 3 a.m. But this time it's different because I realize this happens over and over again so The Almighty Creator can give me another opportunity and another chance, and another, and another, and another.

Summer Hide and Seek
and Fear of the Dark
By Scotti Butler

Summer 1942: World War II was in progress. My dad
was in the Sea Bees, three uncles and a cousin in
the Navy, and two uncles in the US Army Cavalry.
My grandmother had a flag showing five blue stars
hanging in her living room window, a star for every
son serving in the military. My family lived in a large
old-fashioned house in the Oakland Hills (Okay,
so it wasn't "old fashioned" at that time) and I was
in kindergarten. I was learning to play piano on a
beautiful baby grand piano that pretty much filled
the parlor and my brother, Mel, was that adorable
little blue-eyed, freckle-faced, carrot top nicknamed
"Bubbsy" whom everyone adored. I had a cousin
(the one who looked like the Campbell soup baby)
who was called "Punkin" while my nickname was
"Stinkweed."

In retrospect some decades later, I speculated that that nickname was earned by my behavior during those years. For instance, I could recall at age two and a half or so while recuperating from polio and wearing braces on my legs, getting those same braces caught up in the chain-link fence I was attempting to climb, lusting after the ripe fruit in the orange grove near our Long Beach home. Mom would have to come detach me after the friends I had encouraged to climb with me went running to her for help. And then, when I was six or so, I encouraged four or five friends to climb the rose trellis on my grandmother's house in order to jump off of the roof onto the front lawn—repeatedly. I often did things that were disturbing to my family.

The kitchen was one of my favorite rooms that always had interesting and pleasant things happening. An icebox sat against the back wall next to the pantry. The iceman came on a regular basis, bringing a huge block of ice to replace the shrunken block left from the last delivery. The stove was a large black iron, white porcelain-trimmed appliance standing tall on iron legs. It had four burners and a trash burner on one end with an oven and broiler "stack" on the other end. When my teenaged cousin, Diane, occasionally visited she would make a mouth-watering batch of peanut brittle in my mother's biggest cast iron skillet for us to share. I was in awe of her culinary skills and determined to one day match her abilities, at least where peanut-brittle-making was concerned.

A large five-pound can of honey had replaced the sugar bowl on our kitchen table because war-rationing was in effect. My favorite memory is of the mornings we all sat around the table in the dining alcove for breakfast. Mom always threw open the windows to the honeysuckle and baby roses climbing up the outside wall, richly scenting the air while sunshine streamed in.

My parents argued a lot in those days and I was responsible—at least my mind said I was. Mother was so beautiful and had such a bubbly personality that my father was jealous of all the men who admired her when she was at work as a waitress. In the Bay Area during war time, there were lots and lots of servicemen circulating around and the uncles and cousins serving in the Navy were frequent visitors when on leave.

When he was in port, my father watched us kids while mother was at work. This was not a good thing for me one day when I did something my father dis-approved of. He grabbed me by the arm with one hand, grabbed a thick dog collar with the other and proceeded to raise welts on me from my behind down to my ankles and ended by shoving me into a closet and locking the door. He kept me there until Mother came home from work. To this day I haven't a clue what I had done that warranted such violence and I was afraid of the dark for years after. I only knew that something must've been very wrong about me or I wouldn't have warranted such treatment. The good thing was that my father never again laid a violent hand on me after my mother had her say about what he had done. However, it didn't stop the endless verbal abuse.

With five uncles and a couple of cousins in the service, our home was a mecca for each one when on liberty. Our cousin Lyle came to visit while on shore leave one day. My three-year-old brother, Mel, and I were delighted to have an adult who seemed so fun-loving and cheerful. Lyle proposed that we play a game of hide and seek, I would be "it" first and, because Mel was so little, Lyle would help him hide. After counting to 100 by fives, I went looking everywhere, eventually checking out every tree and bush all around the house, even daring the doorway of the dark and scary basement and couldn't find them. Sometime later they came strolling back into the yard, Mel riding on Lyle's shoulder, both of them working on the remnants of ice cream cones. Our cousin had taken Mel to the store down the hill and treated my brother and didn't bring any back for me. My feeling that there surely must be something wrong with me, deepened further. That feeling would become a belief that would deeply influence my life for decades.

The Last to be Happy

By Carl Weber

The room has nothing to say,
And in its silence,
Is still not as soft,
As the man who sits alone.

Memories come to mind,
Of times,
Of paint and makeup,
Grease and color,
Of costumes and hair,
The circus, the tents,
The children laughing at the man.
With appearances as such,
Little it takes,
To see smiles on children,
The joy in hearts.

Not a need for skill,
Nor training or talent.
A wish for love and happiness,
A hope for affection and peace,
Makes any man the expert,
Any, the genius of joy.

But surrounding sights
Prove less mild to memories
And return thoughts to today.
Returning to the man
Who sits alone.
No one near the light,
No one by the heart.
Nothing to do but sit and stare

And still, the room refuses to reply.
The man, blank-eyed,
Has nothing to recall,
But the laughter of the chair,
The smile of the lamp,
The snicker of the walls,
The grin of the table,
Who join with the children,
In laughing at the man.

Lady in Waiting
By Wanda B. Campbell

"Good evening, Miss. Will you be dining alone tonight?" the host asked in an accent I considered too manufactured to be authentic. The pale white skin didn't match the European sound. Oh well, what do I care? If a man who had probably grown up on a farm in Wyoming wants to perpetrate as an Italian, then so be it. I have more important things on my mind tonight. This is the night I have literally waited my entire life for. Nervously, I glance down at the designer watch on my wrist. In less than twenty minutes, I'll come face-to-face with, and experience, the sheer reality of my destiny.

I smile and then answer the gentleman. "No, Mr. Lance Cavanaugh will be joining me shortly."

The host nods then makes a notation on his computer screen before gathering two menus in thin arms and smiles at me. "Follow me, please."

While following my guide to the table I had reserved in the front of the restaurant which allowed an unobstructed view of Piedmont Avenue, I nearly trip over my feet. *You can do this; you've been walking in heels for years,* I remind myself, but my nerves and anxiety cause my legs to wobble anyway. I slowed my pace to keep from falling flat on my face. That's definitely not how I want the distinguished Lance Cavanaugh to see me for the first time; eating carpet with my extra-wide behind in the air.

"Thank you, God," I whisper, after the host hands me a menu. He then leaves me and my nerves alone.

I attempt to read the menu, but my eyes, as if they had a mind of their own, constantly shift to the busy street. I'd picked this table because I wanted the chance to see the man who holds the understanding to my past and the promise of my future in his essence, before he approaches the table. Not that I would readily recognize him, considering we've only talked on the phone a few times. Still, I wanted the advantage of seeing him before he saw me, just in case he's not pleased with my height and weight or the color of my skin and bolts for the front exit.

Not that I'm insecure about what society labels my plus-size frame, short legs, and naturally kinky hair. I look down at my attire and think, maybe I am just a little insecure. Why else would I spend nearly my whole paycheck on a body makeover for this one night? The plain truth: I want, no, I need Lance Cavanaugh to like and want me. I need his affirmation. I thirst for his attention. I crave for his love. I know that is a lot to expect from a man I've never met, but it's the hard truth. I have prayed and fasted about the emptiness in my heart and for an answer God sent Mr. Cavanaugh into my life.

I nod, acknowledging the water and warm bread the waiter places on the table, but I can't eat or drink right now, the man who I pray will love me, the man I have waited all my life for will be here any moment. I am so nervous, I'm not sure I will be able to eat anything at all.

It's not that I'm desperate for a man. At thirty-two, I have had plenty of them. Or shall I say, plenty of men have had me. Not one of the men I shared my body with and opened my heart to cared anything about me. They did, however, have a genuine fondness for my steady paycheck and luxury vehicle, not to mention the freewill offering of my body whenever the collection plate was passed.

There was Tyson, who claimed to be an investment banker, but slept every day until noon. He "loved" me good enough to convince me to fork over $5,000 for some business venture of his and then decided I wasn't the right woman for him. I haven't seen or heard from him since the check cleared the bank.

After sleeping with Jerome for three months and co-signing for him an automobile, he informed me of his decision to reconcile with the wife and kids he conveniently forgot to mention, and had the gall to take the vehicle with him. I should have known something was up when he insisted on purchasing a minivan. I just mailed the last payment two weeks ago.

Now Wayne, he was real slick. We met at Open-Mic night at Yoshi's. That night, he recited a poem about how special I was and I made the mistake of bringing him home. The man was fine with a voice that could put Barry White to shame. Wayne didn't leave my townhouse for six months. He didn't work. He rarely bathed. He did manage to destroy my leather furniture with his cigarettes, wreck my car, and infect me with chlamydia before stealing $3,000 from my savings account. I haven't listened to or read a poem since.

To be fair to the dogs, I mean men, it's not completely their fault they used me up then threw me away like day-old garbage. Since receiving Christ, I have accepted my responsibility. I'm not blind. I am very intelligent. I hold a Master's degree in Psychology and I am currently pursuing my Doctorate. I recognized I was being manipulated, but the void inside of me controlled me. I was so tired of being alone and feeling inadequate. All my life I have felt like something was wrong with me, like I wasn't quite good enough. There was something missing inside me and I thought I could find it in the comfort of men. The phrase, *You're beautiful* or *I'm here for you* had become a drug to me, the toxin that seared my common sense and values.

"Tonight's a new beginning," I tell myself as I once again attempt to read the menu. Lance Cavanaugh is different. He is the answer to my identity, the healing balm for my wounded heart. He will be the first man that I will love with my whole heart. I prayed hard before entering this relationship. Before our brief telephone conversations, I prayed for the right words to say. I asked God to open my ears, so I can recognize the truth. I fasted for three days before arranging this meeting. All of the preparation didn't diminish the deep longing I have for this man to want and love me.

Still oblivious to the contents, I set the menu down and retrieve my compact from my purse. While refreshing my lipstick, I recall the words Lance Cavanaugh had spoken to me during our first phone conversation. "I've been looking for you for years. I thought I would never find you." At first, I thought he was just being polite, but he kept repeating the words. I believed him and now I'm sitting in a restaurant anxiously awaiting a man wearing a black double-breasted suit with a red and black paisley tie.

I return my compact to my purse and direct my attention back to the street while inwardly praying for this evening to be a success. My intuition tells me to turn to the right. I gasp and my heart nearly stops beating. Instantly, my eyes pool with water that glides thick trails down my face. It's him, Lance Cavanaugh. My past, present and future is making quick long deliberate steps toward me. The answer to who I am and the possibilities of who I can become has finally arrived. Slowly and unsteadily I stand.

My visual inspection is quick, but thorough. My hero is not a tall milk-chocolate brother with a washboard stomach. He's short, maybe a couple of inches taller than me with caramel skin that matches mine. No doubt he could pinch more than an inch around his waist, but he wears his clothes well. His head isn't accented with locks or a fresh haircut. He is bald and handsome. In his left hand are a dozen red roses. Like me, he is crying also.

In his wet eyes I see life, my life, and how much more fulfilling my existence will be from this night on. I see joy, excitement, happiness and love. *YES!* I scream inwardly. *He loves me.* I love him too.

He now stands directly in front of me, close enough for me to touch. Unable to control my emotions any longer, my chest heaves and my lips tremble, but I am unable to speak. He places the roses on the table then opens his arms to me. I can't contain myself any longer. The fact that I am standing in a crowded restaurant with strangers gawking at me is not important. My prayers have been answered, my heart is healed and for the first time in my life I feel like a whole person.

"Daddy!" I cry out, throwing my arms around his neck and burying my head against his chest.

"My baby!" he cries back and I feel his tears wash my forehead. He squeezes me tighter. Never have I felt as secure as I do at this moment. Never has my life been so complete.

I have no idea how long we have been standing and holding one another before he reluctantly breaks the embrace. He lifts my chin and with his gentle, yet strong hands removes my tears. He looks directly into eyes that belong to him and gives me what I have waited all my life for.

"I love you," he says. "From this day forward, I want to be part of your life."

"I love you too, Daddy. And I need you in my life so much."

Lance Cavanaugh, my daddy, beams with joy. He hugs me again and kisses my cheek before pulling out my chair. Once seated, he holds my hand and compliments my beauty.

I smile, no, I blush.

Blue Eye Shadow
By Eddrick Jerome

August 24, 1975 was a magical day in my life. I'd just turned eight and had spent the entire summer doing everything that a young boy found interesting. Every day was spent playing various athletic contests throughout my neighborhood. Three flies up, basketball, tag football, and racing my friends on foot or on bikes filled the day. It doesn't get very hot in Richmond, California and I grew up right next to San Pablo Bay. The mild temperature during the day gave way to crisp winds during the evening and the change in temperature always signaled when it was time to go home.

Summer was also vacation time and we'd taken a two-week trip by car down to Southern California to visit relatives in Watts, Inglewood, and to Disneyland. My father always drove, my mother rode shotgun, and my brother sat in the backseat with me. My brother was three years older than me and he ruled the backseat. Imaginary lines were drawn in the middle because I was prone to get on his nerves. Once, when he was sleeping, I found an old French fry under the front seat. I picked it up and placed it by his mouth. Instinctively he gobbled it up and I laughed so loud I woke him up. He never knew what happened, but he instinctively knew that I crossed the line. So he banished me back to the other side of the car.

I had no idea that August 24, 1975 would change my life. My only priority was gearing up for another spectacular season of kickball at Bayview elementary school. I was a star in kickball, normally the first pick even in the second grade. My third-grade season was going to be historic. There were two playgrounds at Bayview, one for grades one through three, and a larger one for grades four through six. I'd kicked eight "round the world" homeruns in the second grade. These were true homeruns that cleared the fence in right field of the kickball blacktop in the small yard. Joey Marazzo held the record of twelve in a single school year. And he did it in third grade. My focus was to smash the record and add my name to the annals of kickball history. It was within my reach.

August 24, 1975 started out like all other days that summer. My friends and I rode our bikes out to Plum Country in the middle of the day. Plum Country was a patch of fruit trees in the middle of Point Pinole Park, which was adjacent to Parchester Village where I grew up. The Atlas Powder Company, which made gun powder, was originally located a few miles within the regional park. The owners of the company built grand Victorian homes on the property. The company shut down in the forties and the houses were torn down. But they'd planted a series of fruit trees that bloomed all spring and summer. We'd pick and eat plums, black berries, apples, and other delicious fruit until our bellies well full. Who knew that we were riding our bikes through gun powder tailings and shit. But that fruit was amazing on a mild summer day.

As I said, that day was like others. I knew that my parents were going out for the evening. They belonged to a club named the Searchers, a collective of people from the Black Arkansas Diaspora. The Northern California branch held various events each year and this event was scheduled to be in Oakland. My parents had no qualms about leaving us at home alone. It was a different time and I have no memory whatsoever of having a babysitter. Sometimes we would spend the night at my aunt's who lived a couple of blocks away. I came in for the day around five-thirty and they were already getting prepared to go out.

My parents usually bought something special to eat for my brother and I when they were going out. To my utter joy there was a hot Straw Hat pizza waiting for us. My brother and I ate the pizza like royalty at a feast. I washed the pizza down with a cold Shasta Creme Soda. Life was great for this eight-year-old boy.

I watched my dad walk from the bathroom to the bedroom in his drawers. We had no sisters, so he had no problem walking around the house like that. My parents were very stylish in both dress and bearing. He'd laid out a dark-brown suit and yellow floral-print shirt. Yes, the shirt had the wide collars typical of shirts from that era. He was fond of Stacy Adams shoes and the brown two-tone shoes he picked were a perfect choice (I still wear Stacy Adams to this day). This may have been the time when he dabbled with an earring; all I remember is that he would take it out whenever we went to see my old-school grandmother.

My mother was resplendent in an orange sleeveless dress. Rufus and Chaka Khan's "Tell Me Something Good" was playing on the radio. She was sitting in front of the mirror applying her makeup. Women wore the clip-on hair pieces back then and hers was flawless. My mother was a very beautiful woman and my friends frequently told me how lucky I was. I came up to her just to give her a hug. She leaned over and kissed me on the forehead and then shooed me away so that she could apply her eye shadow. It was Technicolor blue, typical of the kind used in the seventies. She was an expert in applying it.

My parents were a striking couple. We weren't rich by any means, but my dad's job at the oil refinery kept us housed, fed, clothed, and a nice car in the driveway. I never lacked for anything growing up and I am thankful for that. The memory of them admiring themselves in the mirror that night is with me today. I took a film class years later in college and that image is what film buffs would call "mis en scene". Look it up.

The time came for them to leave. As usual, my dad couldn't leave without fixing a drink first. Johnnie Walker Red on ice was his drink of choice. My mom hugged my brother and me. My dad escorted her by the arm and they walked out to the banana-yellow Cadillac El Dorado sitting in the driveway. My mother held his drink as he got in. Right before he started the car he lit a cigarette. With drink in hand and cigarette in his lips they drove off for an evening of socializing and dancing.

I closed the door and locked it. When I turned around my brother had gone to our room. I headed for the den to watch TV. But first I went to the kitchen and popped open another cold can of crème soda. I got to the den and settled in for a night of network comedy. About twenty minutes went by and I noticed that my brother had not joined me. My big brother and I had a bond that was unbreakable even though I got on his nerves. He was my guide, protector, and truly looked out for me. My parents made it a point to remind me that he was in charge whenever they left us alone.

Another ten minutes went by so I went to look for him. He wasn't in our room, nor was he in the kitchen. I walked back down the hall and noticed that my parents' bedroom door was closed. Now, I admit that nothing gave me more excitement than rummaging through my father's chifforobe, which is what he called his armoire, when they were gone. He kept various types of cologne on the top and I would play with watches, rings, key chains, and other stuff that would keep the attention of an eight-year-old boy.

I approached the door and opened it slightly. What I saw took my breath away and left me standing with my mouth open. There, sitting at the same makeup mirror that my mother had used earlier, was my eleven-year-old big brother. He turned to face me and to my surprise he was fully made up in my mom's makeup. Foundation, eye-liner, lipstick, and the bluest eye shadow in the world. He'd even gone into her stash of hair pieces and clipped one to the back of his head. I was silent, which was very hard for me. But we didn't need to speak to understand the gravity of the situation. He was my big brother, so I knew not to joke or make fun because he would have kicked my ass, even in full makeup.

I didn't understand what I was seeing. I couldn't comprehend the image of what I was seeing. He knew that I was in a state of shock so he calmly arose from the makeup table and walked up to me. It appeared that he had been studying my mother because his makeup was fabulous, a word I learned later in life but fit this situation perfectly.

"You want to watch *Sanford and Son*?" I asked with a dry mouth.

"Sure," he said. And we walked to the den. He sat on the couch and I sat on the loveseat. It was as if this was the most normal thing in the world. My eleven-year-old brother and I sat and laughed at the show. Me in a SF Giant's tee shirt, tough skin pants from Sears, and green Chuck Taylors. My brother in Lee jeans, a red button down shirt and cosmetic-counter-quality makeup.

I would steal a glance every now and then just to see if he was still made up. He caught me looking at him once or twice, but he didn't care. He knew that I would never betray what I was seeing. That was the type of bond we had. In fact, this is the first time that I am revealing what happened on August 24, 1975. I never told my parents.

I didn't know anything about gay and lesbian lifestyles back then. It was not something that was remotely within my consciousness as an eight-year-old. I had no label to use and no words to articulate my feelings or my observations of my brother. But this was the day that I learned that he was different and my perspective of him changed. He was my brother, so there were no freak show connotations or anything like that. My big brother was as tough as any boy in our neighborhood and kids usually left him alone and stayed on his good side.

About an hour later he went back into my parents' bedroom and returned to the den in his normal appearance. Gone was the makeup and hair piece. We continued watching television until it was time to go to bed. He made me go to bed when it was time because he was in charge.

My brother didn't officially come out as gay until 1988, long after we had moved out of the house. During the years leading up to that he led what some would call a "normal" life. He ran track, broke bones playing high school football, and took girls to the prom. Yes, sometimes I would get the "Why yo' brother act like that?" questions, but I brushed them off like a protective little brother was supposed to do. I knew the truth, but it was something that only we shared.

The ravages of HIV and AIDS decimated young black men in the Bay Area during the late eighties and early nineties. Sadly, my brother was infected with this insidious disease and we lost him in 1995 after a long and painful demise. He died two days after my first daughter was born so he was never able to see her grow up into the smart, confident, bright young woman that she is today. Had it not been for my loving wife and beautiful child I would have spiraled after losing him. His spirit is with me today and I reflect on the amazing time we had together. He never suffered from dementia and remained clear-minded and funny up until the end. One of the last things he said to me was, "I don't hate God or blame God. This is my fate and I am comfortable with the next chapter." Who knew that seeing him as a child in blue eye shadow would emotionally prepare me for losing him. I miss you, EJO II.

Chocolate Ecstasy
By C.L. Miles

Our midnight moments spent together are pure erotic pleasure. I wake up in the morning next to you, wondering why my face and hair are sticky. I feel guilty while pouring my coffee knowing I'm not working toward my goal with my weight. Although I suffer for my love, I know I'm not the only sinner when it comes to you.

I lose track of time during the day, dreaming of you. There are few minutes available during the day with no interruptions, when the two of us can share that special moment together in total bliss. I can't get enough of your milking sensation. You melt in my mouth and in my hands. With your nuttiness, we are a match meant to be. I'm koo-koo for cocoa butter.

Your sweet pure cane sugar with a touch of soy milk, including the added fat, give you the right number of calories (per serving). Even now, your rich body of natural flavors and aromatic essences, sends clouds of satisfaction and new experiences through my soul. My mouth waters with overwhelming thoughts of addiction. One piece is never enough.

Guilty once again. I lust for a piece of heaven. Holding your thick dark life's blood in my grasp, I anticipate the smooth melting glide down my throat. You are simply more than I can imagine or deserve. You have so many flavors, it's hard to choose which one I love best. Only by adding almonds can perfection be improved.

I'm addicted to your luscious dark sugary taste. Having you hot with whipped cream and gooey marshmallows is a special treat. I can't survive without you. I dream about swimming in a huge milk-chocolate vat. Everything about you makes my mouth water and my heart pump faster. I can never get enough of you. For me Hershey's, your milk chocolate is the nectar of life.

Flooding Forward
By Roger Oberbeck

Roy Bekker, a Nuclear Test Engineer at Mare Island Naval Shipyard, was boarding the newly constructed Nuclear Submarine USS Guitarro tied up to the seawall at about 8 PM, the start of the swing shift lunch period. He noticed that the submarine was lower than normal from the top of the seawall and the gangplank had an abnormally steep angle down to the hull of the sub. Must be a really low tide tonight, he thought.

Roy relieved another nuclear test engineer directing a test in the lower-level Auxiliary Machinery Room Number 2 (AMR2) just aft of the Reactor Compartment.

FLOODING FORWARD! FLOODING FORWARD! blared over the submarine's address system. The submarine lurched down to a 10-degree angle by the bow. "Wow, definitely flooding forward, I wonder if the submarine is sinking?" Roy declared.

The sailor operating the valves turned to him and said, "What should we do?"

"Shut those valves and get out of here."

The other two on-shift nuclear test engineers immediately left the compartment and went topside to check on the flooding.

Roy stayed in the AMR2 lower level for a few minutes to secure the test and then went up one level and back to the Engine Room and entered the Maneuvering Room. The normally crowded Maneuvering Room was deserted, except for the Shutdown Reactor Operator, who was staring worriedly at the Reactor Plant Control Panel. The Engineering Officer of the Watch (EOOW), normally stationed in Maneuvering, was not present. Roy checked to make sure the main coolant pumps, big 480 Volt 3 phase pumps, were secured, because he didn't want them energized if the reactor compartment flooded. The main coolant pumps were all secured.

Roy went to the reactor compartment and climbed up a temporary ladder to the top of the hull via the opening left in the hull over the reactor compartment to install the nuclear core. The submarines hull was under water to the sail, which meant the forward escape hatch was under several feet of water. The two other engineers were at the Weapons Loading Hatch forward of the reactor compartment, pulling hoses and cable out of the hatch. Roy joined them and looked down the hatch and saw several feet of water flowing through the passageway. They continued to try to clear the hoses and cables out of the hatch.

Somebody up on the seawall kept yelling, "Hey, you guys, you better get off of there, that's dangerous." While they were working, Roy noticed a Shop 38 Marine Machinist walking past them from forward, trying to look inconspicuous. They got all but one cable out of the hatch. Roy was standing with his back to the bow, when suddenly he noticed that his right foot was getting wet. He looked down and saw that the hull was under water to where he was standing. He realized that they could do nothing more, and left the submarine by climbing the gangplank, which was now vertical instead of horizontal.

Roy called the Nuclear Test Division management and told them that the Guitarro was sinking. The Joint Test Group Chairman, Vic Andrews, would not believe him, he kept saying, "Ah, come on, Roy, you're kidding me."

"Damn it, Vic," Roy finally said, "the Guitarro is sunk."

Roy went back down to where the Guitarro was berthed and observed that the entire hull was under water several feet, and there was a large dimple in the water over the reactor access patch. Every thirty seconds or so a large geyser of muddy water would shoot about twenty feet in the air as air bubbles from the reactor compartment would escape. Roy noticed two men running forward from the Engine Room escape hatch through knee-deep water. They were the Nuclear Ship Superintendent and a Nuclear Electrician who had went back into the submarine to make sure everybody had gotten off. The submarine had sunk during the swing shift lunch period, so most of the shipyard workers had left the ship. The ship's watch section had abandoned ship by orders of the EOOW, passed over the sound-powered phone system. The primary plant was in a solid plant condition with pressure being controlled by a Charging Station Watch and a Discharge Station Watch in the lower level AMR2, both on sound-powered phones. These Watches never received the "abandon ship" order, as water was already pouring down the bulkhead between the Reactor Compartment and AMR2, and had shorted out the sound-powered phone system. Their lives were saved because the Leading Petty Officer of the watch mustered his watch section to the dock and realized he was missing two of his watchstanders. He went back into the sinking submarine and got the watchstanders off the ship before it sunk.

Roy's last duty was to write the Shift Test Engineer Log with the entry that Nuclear Testing was secured as the Guitarro sank. The nuclear test they were conducting required zero list and trim on the submarine. Before the non-nuclear test group trimmed the submarines by using a formal test procedure documenting levels in tanks. all hull openings and required weights needed if necessary to achieve zero list and trim.

The Shipyard Production Officer, a Naval Captain (second in command of the shipyard) decided that it was too expensive to have a Technical Division trim the submarine and ordered the outboard Marine machine shop trim the ship. However, he neglected to ensure that they were properly trained on how to trim a ship.

The day shift machine shop foreman said that the submarine had a down angle but the swing shift machine shop foreman checked the trim and was sure he had an up angle, and had the trim tank pumped from aft to forward. The trim was measured with a scope called a Gunner's Transit, sighting on a graduated brass plate on the Torpedo Room bulkhead.

The swing shift foreman didn't realize that the scope inverted the image and the submarine was already at a down angle. He then made the fatal mistake of violating a red danger tag on the ballast tank vent valve, broke the lock on the vent valve and proceeded to fill the ballast tank with a seawater fire hose, which has a flow rate of about 125 gallons per minute. A security watch warned them several times that the submarine's draft had decreased, but they replied, "Don't bother us, we know what we're doing."

When the submarine became lower in the water, waters started spilling into the open manway into the sonar dome (the manway cover had been removed by persons unknown, but no cofferdam had been installed around the opening). When the sonar dome flooded it pulled the bow down and water started pouring in the forward escape hatch, flooding the forward compartment. All of the submarine's watertight doors were blocked with cables and hoses, preventing them from being closed. Consequently, none of the compartments could be secured to stop the flooding. A basic principle of submarine design is if the ballast tank is filled the submarine submerges. It is a bad idea if the hatches are open, there are hull patches missing, and watertight doors cannot be closed. Sure enough, the Guitarro sank.

The Navy brought in a salvage team with divers that went into the sunken submarine and cut all the hoses and cables that were blocking the watertight doors and welded patches on any bulkhead openings. Large cofferdams were installed over the escape hatches and the reactor compartment hull patch opening. The reactor compartment was then pumped out.

The Nuclear Test Engineers had calculated, based on the temperature of the main coolant system, and the temperature of the water in the Napa River. The main coolant system pressure would have decreased to a twenty-four-inch vacuum. Two nuclear test pipefitters volunteered to go into the reactor compartment, with the submarine still sunken, and install a compound gauge (indicating both pressure and vacuum) on the primary plant's high point vent valve. When the vent valve was open the gauge indicated that the primary plant had a twenty-four-inch vacuum. This was good news as it meant that the primary plant had zero leakage, and Napa River water at the shipyard was about one third saltwater (about 5000 ppm chlorides), which is very bad for stainless steel, causing chloride stress corrosion.

The remaining compartments were pumped out slowly and carefully and the Guitarro returned to the surface on Sunday at noon. It had been sunk for approximately sixty-four hours. The restoration would take approximately two years.

The Navy Production Officer tried to shift the blame for the sinking of the Guitarro to the Nuclear Test Division, with the argument that by blowing down the tank they had been testing, it would raise the aft end of the submarine, thereby forcing the bow down under water and flooding the forward compartment. He had evidently convinced the Armed Forces subcommittee that this was the case, because when Roy was called to the Shipyard Commander's office to testify, the Congressman did not ask him any questions about what happened when the Guitarro sank, but repeatedly tried to get him to agree that blowing down the tank would raise the aft of the submarine and force the bow underwater. Roy told him several times that that was not the way it worked. Finally, the Congressman said, "Don't you think it could have been the straw that broke the camel's back?"

Furious, Roy yelled, "If that damned submarine could have been sunk by a damn straw, it was in pretty damn bad shape."

The stenographer stopped typing, there was dead silence for a moment then the Congressman said, "No further questions."

The formal Naval Board of Inquiry investigating the sinking of the Guitarro determined that blowing down the tank undergoing testing would have raised the entire submarine three-sixteenths of an inch, and they determined that the Navy Production Officer and the Shipyard Commander were primarily responsible for the sinking of the Guitarro.

Several months later the swing shift Marine machine shop foreman that broke the lock and the ballast tank vent valve and filled the ballast tank with the seawater fire hose was found dead in his closed garage where his car had been running.

The TV program *Rowan and Martin's Laugh-In* awarded Mare Island Naval Shipyard the "Fickle Finger of Fate Award" for sinking the Guittaro.

An Ode to Married Life

By Linda Dogué Holliman

My husband makes me happy,
Sometimes he makes me mad.
He fills my days with laughter,
He holds me when I'm sad.

He tells me that I'm beautiful,
He tells me that I'm smart.
He treats me like a princess,
He sees inside my heart.
He leads our kids to Glory
With his Bible in his hand.
He demonstrates life's lessons
So that they understand.

He's strong and wise and thoughtful,
And, yes, he's pretty hot!
He's quite the studly athlete,
He gives it all he's got.
A chef he's not, but that's OK,
He's charmed by my cuisine.
He'll gladly do the dishes
And wipe the kitchen clean.

I really love to travel.
At home he'd rather be.
Thanks to i-technology
He's always next to me.
That's if, of course, before my trip
The kids set up our Skype,
And messaging, and Facebook.
Now, if only I could type!

He thinks I can do anything,
He's my biggest fan.
The love we share is from above.
God's blessed me with this man.

See You Later, MyAngel

By Wanda B. Campbell

In memory of my granddaughter

On Sunday, November 2, 2014, my grand-daughter, MyAngel Kaymar entered the world at 1:53 a.m. She didn't announce her arrival with a high-pitched scream or wail like her twin sister did sixteen minutes prior. Instead, she made a quiet subtle entrance. Then she wailed.

We'd known for months MyAngel wouldn't be with us long. The doctors had delivered the news during the first trimester of my daughter's pregnancy, yet I hoped for a different outcome. As a woman of faith, I prayed until I heard the still small voice confirm the doctor's prognosis. Then I accepted the pending outcome.

Sunday afternoon as I rocked MyAngel in my arms inside the NICU, with the feel of her tiny fingers wrapped around my pinky, I closed my eyes and mentally shared precious memories with her. I imagined MyAngel scooting around on the carpet in our family room. I saw her attempting to take steps and reaching for the glass figurines on my living room table. I felt her patting my arm and calling me Mimi. I envisioned my husband flying her in the air, as he'd done my daughter so many years ago. I saw joy radiating from her as she showed me the latest masterpiece she'd made at school. I saw us shopping together and me teaching her the recipe to my famous chocolate chip cookies. I saw so many things.

Then I began singing the words to one of my favorite songs, "It Is Well". I chose that song because although the pain of letting MyAngel go is indescribable, I know she's going to a better place and one day I'll see her again. I sang until no more tears were left. Then I stroked her face and kissed her cheek and said, "See you later, MyAngel."

Good-Bye
By Naomi Connor

In memory of I.J.J.

I stood there next to you, holding my breath; waiting. Waiting for you to open your eyes. You, almost startled in amazement as to why I was so close to you. I stood there in your personal space. Waiting. Waiting for you to roll your eyes and laugh at me for being sentimental. I stood there next to you with many others present. The room was full. There were prayers, hushed voices, machines humming. I stood there next to you; waiting. Waiting for your breath to be in rhythm with mine.

Weeks before, our conversations had been casual. It wasn't weird for us to talk about caskets or burial plots. Texas is a big state and I might as well be buried on my own property. I had to talk about it with you 'cause Honeyman wasn't having this conversation with me. We discussed funerals as if conversing about the scene in *Imitation of Life*. I can't remember which version was your favorite.

I brought with me a mixture of essential oils to massage you. I figured that the aroma would relax and calm me and maybe you, too. I needed to talk to you. I was communicating with you with my hands. I smoothed my hands about you as a mother would caress her child. I smiled and talked to you at times. Your man told me to be sure to get that rough spot on your baby toe.

I'm waiting to hear you talk to me about the train trip that we are planning for New Orleans. It's your idea, so work out the details. That thing that you have about Martha's Vineyard, well, I'm game for that, too. You should know that I'm not parading all of my goodness in a swimsuit in public. Okay, maybe a one-piece suit. How about you? What about that plan to go to Italy? That's a lot of walking. Are you up to it? Are we taking the guys or are we going to do that one on our own?

The lavender, rosemary and sweet orange fragrances all dance around our noses. A light cloud of optimism. A soon-to-be-distant reminder. I knew that you didn't have a problem with lavender, but there was a voice of discord. You know me…it didn't matter. And, yes, I did remember the rough spot on your right baby toe.

I'm enjoying the smell of the essential oils as I think it may be all that I'm going to be able to keep. I'm still being patient. I'm still waiting for you to open your eyes and laugh at me. I hear you commenting on how smooth the oil makes your skin feel. I can hear your Honey laughing at me for giving you the "spa" treatment. I'm still waiting for you to open your eyes.

Your Honey is swimming alone. The kids are quiet. Young Man is keeping to himself. Young Woman, while distracted, is holding her own. The kids are young and hopefully resilient. This is demanding at any age. This journey is new to all of us.

I keep thinking, Thy will be done. I notice that I repeat this more and more in my mind and especially when I feel defeated. As hard as I try, life has taught me something that I must share with the family. You told us that everything was going to be okay. We listened, but nothing has made this easy. Tears still flow of which we have no control. At times, the cloud seems to catch us all at once. We miss you.

Not that I've given up, but it's time to say goodbye. I waited for you to open your eyes and had to accept Thy will. My time with you now is limited. I will cry for the trips that we can't travel together and the calls that can no longer be made. There is a wedding in the works and I'm sure you won't miss it. The grandkids that are sure to come are going to miss your cooking. I can't remember the broccoli-rice casserole recipe. Daughter is getting together some of the recipes for me. There are so many incomplete things.

As busy as I always seem, I'm feeling that the more that I crowd into my day, the less I will miss you. My projects to help others, spending more time with the family, appreciating the little things in life, finding time to be happy; these are all things that I cherish. Then I stop. I remember. I cry. Then I look forward to another day.

Never Forgotten

By Rita "em" Emery

You no longer greet us as we unlock your cage door.

You're no longer there to eat your treats of cherries
and grapes.

You're not there to make us smile, make us laugh.

You're no longer there to walk until both of us drop
from fatigue.

You were a family member here at the Suisun
Wildlife Center.

You were a friend to all the volunteers, a loving soul
the community will never forget.

You taught us all you were a great wildlife
ambassador to the marsupial species.

It will take time to heal, for silence to go away.

POGO, you'll always be near, loved, missed and
    forever in our hearts

The Killing of An Old Man

By Carl Weber

Two doors down from a memory
A small child plays with sticks and balls,
Goes running, jumping,
Around the park.
And bicycles go cycling, turning, speeding.
Children gather with teams and voices,
And through the shouts and laughter,
Some turn to home with sadness,
Some turn to ice cream with gladness.

Across the street from forgotten thoughts,
A grown man drives to think and ponder.
Strives to gain, forever missing,
What he wants and where he's going.
Slows down the car,
Never really knowing.
Sees in a park,
A child's cycling, sticks and balls.
Hears shouts and laughter no longer there.

Around the corner of a changed mind
An old man walks with a fragile cane,
Though the cane walks faster than he.
And with his body of aching joints,
He nods and shakes to a park bench.
And becomes a watcher,
Of slowed-down cars with mindful drivers.

For in just a moment,
He leans to the right and falls,
While others think he sleeps.
But the old man died,
And got up,
And walked away with sticks and balls,
With a child's laughter running free.

To Pee or Not to Pee

C.L. Miles

There is nothing more uncomfortable than when you are driving down a deserted stretch of highway with a full bladder. I should know, it's happened more often than I care to say. But I know I'm not the only woman this has happened to.

Guys have it easy. They can pull over anywhere, face away from the road, whip it out and go. No questions asked. Women, women have to make a production of untying, unzipping, pulling and who knows what else. Not to mention we have to worry about some freak or animal jumping out of the bushes as our hands are busy holding cloth away from our bodies and not available for defense.

Driving US Route 50 at dusk, heading southeast toward Moab, Utah, for a long overdue vacation with six hours left in the journey. There were no visible lights or life in any direction for miles. I knew I should not have had that last cup of coffee before leaving Reno, NV. Coffee had always gone right though me and the sign I just passed stated, *421 miles* to the next gas station. With no restroom in sight and none in the immediate future, what alternative did I have.

I was in trouble. The urge was overwhelming me and I knew I couldn't hold it anymore. Trying not to panic, I took the chance and pulled off the side of the road, with only the cactus as a witness. In hindsight, I should have just peed in my pants and kept driving down that lonely dark road toward some hidden town. Just when relief was insight and the point of no return, a car pulled over. Too late. No choice but to finish what had already begun.

How could I know my embarrassment had just started? The crunch of gravel beneath the weight of boots came closer. Suddenly, those big boots stood directly in my line of sight. I stared in horror at the man in uniform. Caught with my pants around my ankles, no explanation was necessary. He grinned and then retreated. I had just unwillingly added to the officer's stories for gossip and laughs.

I had no dignity left. I took strength in the fact that I knew I wasn't the first nor the last to be caught with my pants down.

The Deal
By Anita L. Robertson

I did it. I made the deal. He didn't answer the phone.
God did not show up to the bargaining table, but
Lucifer did. He sat there, quiet and innocuous, a
short balding man with a round, pleasant face—a
face that you could easily have sitting across from
you during Sunday dinner. His rosy cheeks and red
nose seemed to exude warmth of heart, but were no
doubt the result of the heat that seemed to radiate
from him. It was indeed warm, and I found myself
taking off my down-filled coat, a necessity for the
bone-chilling weather outside. Although I had shed
my outer apparel, it was evident that he was not
bothered by the rise in temperature. He looked comfortable despite his many layers: a well-worn tweed
jacket, under which a brown, wool vest covered a
camel-colored shirt. He gestured for me to sit across
from him at the card table which was in the center
of the room, and I complied. He remained silent,
opened his briefcase and took out a single document.

It struck me, the simplicity of it all. That one document, illuminated by a single light which hung from the rafters, in a dark warehouse with only the dust-covered boxes sitting around us as our mute witnesses. If they could speak, what secrets would they reveal about the countless transactions of the men, women and children who sat in this room, desperate for solace? Looking down I pondered these clients' situations and wondered if the cigarette butts, which were strewn all over the concrete floor, were a sign of anxiety or apprehension. Did even a single soul give a second thought to what they were about to enter into?

It had happened so quickly. That one phone call to God, unanswered by Him or any of his representatives, which had automatically redirected to the services of Lucifer Inc., who wanting the business, answered the call himself. I was looking for God and did he know where He could be reached? I inquired.

"No. No, God here," he said.

"That number has been derelict for quite some time, perhaps He never made good on His payments. But I would be more than happy to help you. I guarantee relief from your troubles and have the power to grant wishes, however grandiose they may appear. Now, how may I aid you?" his velvety voice resumed. Although the phone became hot in my hand and desperation forced my tolerance, I carried on.

"Well, I definitely need help. You're my last resort," I stammered.

We agreed to meet the next day, at his insistence. Although he preferred to meet with me on the eve of this initial conversation, I impressed upon him my necessity to fulfill my maternal duties and could not. We set up a time and a place where we could discuss my plight and what I would pay in return for his remedy.

So here we met, at a deserted warehouse down by the wharf an hour or so bus ride from the bustle of my suburbia. It was eerily quiet, the only evidence of life presenting itself when the dead air was cut briefly by the two mongrel dogs who ran down the side alley. Their silhouettes and breath outlined by the moonlight, their exuberance not a quest for mischief but perhaps a veiled search for comfort. It was also 9:00 pm and no one knew I was here. Lucifer demanded secrecy.

Having regained my sense of time and thinking I smelled smoke. I looked back up from the floor at Lucifer, who was studying the fine print of the document. So, I resumed my scrutiny of the surroundings, checking for the dubious fire, but quickly became cognizant of the rapidly increasing temperature. It was now hot, and I was forced to roll my sleeves up and wave my hand feverishly across my face for some relief. But Lucifer still sat there, dry and unfazed by the sweltering conditions encroaching upon us. Even the beads of water that had formed high up on the fogged-up windows were running down, trying to escape into the cracks on the floor. Lucifer, aware but unmoved by my discomfort looked at me with his beady eyes. I could see that those eyes, steadily shifting like those of a chameleon were deep like black holes, absorbing everything but emitting nothing. He was not readable and I, as obvious as a bad poker player trying to fool the house. I remembered who I was dealing with. Then he spoke.

"You said you were desperate," Lucifer stated in a voice that was soft and unassuming.

"Ah ya," I said, taken aback. "You are Lucifer, aren't you? You sound very different than the guy I spoke with yesterday."

"I assure you that it is me, madam. Because I deal with people from every walk of life, gender and age, I customize my presentation based on their needs. So, you said you were desperate?" he reiterated.

"Yes. It's my son. He was born with a serious medical condition. I've taken him to see so many different doctors and none of them could help him, except a little. They all told me that treatment is limited and he's not gonna have a good quality of life. At first, I didn't want to believe them but after doing so much research and trying so hard to get help, I think they're right. He's only eight. I really need your help, I'll do anything."

"For centuries I have been helping mothers like yourself," he replied.

"What can you do for him?" I whimpered.

"Why, I can restore the good life that he was robbed of at birth," he said, smiling with a twinkle in his eyes.

"But how?"

"I use bought souls, as their power and depth are endless, they are timeless and perpetual, a perfect resource to be harnessed by someone who appreciates their value. Someone special like myself." Snickering he added, "One pays one's goodwill ahead."

"Why do you do this? What's in it for you?" I asked.

"Like any successful businessman, I take a cut. Furthermore, my deals are forged in fire and I guarantee one-hundred percent delivery."

"So, payment is my soul upon my death?" In my query for clarification, I could feel apprehension grip my being and I looked down at the dead cigarette butts. Diverting my eyes did not ease Lucifer's increasingly penetrating presence and I looking back up, waited meekly for his answer.

"Yes, my tormented madam, it shall be mine upon your death, whenever that may be," his voice conveying empathy. "A small, small price to have your child live in normalcy and happiness."

He continued, "Tell me about your precious son. Does he desire such things as riding a bike with his friends to the store for candy, or fishing in a lake with his father? Do you want him to have companionship and grow old, surrounded by grandchildren?"

He pressed on, asking me questions about my son's condition, pulling out details which were becoming more painful to bear with each successive inquiry until I, not being able to handle my exploding heart, broke down in a mess of agony. I was not in control. The heat was unbearable and there was the distinct smell of burning flesh. Even the room seemed to glow crimson through my tear-filled eyes.

"Please, I'll do anything. I'll sign your contract," I begged.

Pulling a quill out of his jacket, Lucifer quickly grabbed my finger, stating triumphantly, "My deals are non-revocable once signed."

His predatory eyes paralyzed me, and I immediately felt like a caught mouse in a cat's game. The quill came down determined on my finger and my blood dripped out onto the contact, sealing the deal. Phantom flames momentarily engulfed the room. Lucifer laughed a demonic laugh and morphed into a beast that only hell could produce. He disappeared into the floor taking everything hot with him, leaving only biting cold.

In complete shock of what just befell, I lingered, my sweat now feeling like millions of ice needles growing in my skin. Feeling for my coat, I put it on and reviewed the interaction from a nightmare-like state. Did this really just happen? Am I dreaming? Where did the table and Lucifer go? I soon realized what had brought me here, but did it really transpire?

I felt my way out of the warehouse, my eyes traumatized by the intensity of the light contrasts that had been executed against them. Staggering on trembling legs to the bus stop and feeling nauseated at the possibility of the truth, I rounded the corner and stepped off the curb. I heard a screech and felt my body being propelled through the air.

"Pain. Intense pain. Can't move. A man's yelling. Panicked. There's Lucifer. He's coming for me."

Sweet Macanudo

By Eddrick Jerome

"Ladies and gentlemen the captain has switched on the seatbelt sign and we will land at Hartsfield-Jackson Airport in Atlanta in about fifteen minutes. Please move your seat to the upright position…"

Cyntal peered out the window of the plane, trying to catch a glimpse of the Atlanta skyline. All the years of hard work, sacrifice, and studying had paid off. Two days before she received her master's degree, Cyntal was offered a managerial position at Coca-Cola's headquarters in Atlanta. The offer included a signing bonus, company car, and a nice apartment. Her dreams had come true.

She tried to control her emotions. She was getting too excited. Cyntal pulled out a business magazine that featured African-American business profiles and financial advice. She quickly thumbed through the pages. An ad for Macanudo cigars caught her attention. Cyntal was surprised that a woman was depicted savoring a large brown cigar with wisps of smoke and a glowing orange tip. The fine sister in the ad was dressed in a high-end business suit and had that head tilted smiley look that models exhibit when they're faking having fun. But the ad was effective.

Cyntal was twenty-six, educated and beautiful. She was a shade less than five-feet-seven in flat shoes. The struggle for the soul of America was visible in her features. The spice of distant Spanish descent was wrapped in a deep-caramel African coating, which had simmered with random European inflection. She was poised and articulate yet her undeniable urban roots hadn't been lost. Cyntal was exactly what American idealism offered.

The plane landed and she eagerly got her bags. She noticed all of the black folks working in the airport. She'd read about Atlanta being the black capital of the South and she was finally seeing it up close. Several fellas offered to assist her with her bags but she politely declined. Cyntal was always ready to do things for herself.

Twenty-four hours earlier Cyntal was a college student in L.A. with ice water and three hot dogs in her refrigerator. Now she strolled confidently through the airport with keys to a company car. Cyntal passed by a tobacco store in the heart of the airport. She stopped and remembered the way the woman in the ad made her feel, so she went into the store. Five minutes later she emerged with a small box of Macanudos.

She got lost on the way to the apartment. It took about an hour longer than it should have. The apartment was on the third floor of a modern building.

Once inside, she giggled, kicked off her shoes, and inspected all three bedrooms. The carpeting was thick and plush. It felt smooth to her bare feet. It was just before the evening hour and she was tired from the trip. Coca-Cola had stocked the fridge with all kinds of food and goodies. And the bar was also well-equipped.

She took a shower which washed away some of the euphoria of her new situation. The enormity of the change in her life came down on her. For a moment she became scared and shed a tear or two. But it didn't last long. Cyntal had met and conquered many challenges in her short life. By the time she finished drying off, with the heaviest towel she'd ever felt, her moment of uncertainty had passed. She dressed in a pair of cotton boxer shorts with a long sheer pajama top over them.

Cyntal opened the freezer and took out a frozen dinner. She decided to have a drink and listen to music while her food heated up. With drink in hand, Cyntal went to the sliding glass doors that lead out onto the balcony. She could see her reflection in the glass. Cyntal looked at herself for a long time. She tried to look serious and business-oriented. Then she remembered the lady in the ad. She went over to the counter and opened the box of cigars. She took one out and cut the end with the free cutter that came with the purchase. Cyntal gulped down the rest of the drink and moved right next to the glass door. She placed the cigar between her fingers just like the model and held it up to her lips. She looked at herself in the door again and this time she *felt* business-like.

She decided to smoke the cigar but didn't want the smell in her apartment. So she opened the sliding door and stepped out on the balcony.

There was a slight breeze, but the weather was nice. It took her three flicks of the lighter to light the cigar and when she took the first hit she coughed violently. There was more smoke than she anticipated so she closed the sliding door. Cyntal positioned herself by the railing and gazed out at Atlanta. Her fascination with the Macanudo began to wane and Cyntal became light- headed. The smoke was making her eyes water. She stubbed the cigar out after about five puffs and went back to the sliding door. To her horror, it was locked!

Panic swept over her as she desperately tried to open the door. She tugged and pulled on the handle, but it wouldn't budge. The last light of the day crept away from the balcony. Cyntal realized that she was trapped. She looked over the balcony and down to the street below. The noise from the evening's rush-hour traffic drowned out her attempts to call out for help. Cyntal walked over to the door again. The breeze became cooler and she shivered for the first time.

After five hard tugs on the door she began to cry. Her first night in Atlanta had been tarnished by a temporary diversion from her core self. Cyntal was definitely not the woman in the ad. She learned a quick lesson about being herself and staying true to her own tastes. Cigars? Never again.

Cyntal stopped crying and started thinking. There was an old rag tied to a chair on the balcony. She removed the rag and stepped to the edge of the balcony. Cyntal took the lighter from her pajama pocket and lit the rag on fire. She swung the rag around her head a few times until the flames moved quickly up the rag. Her action worked. Someone across the street called the fire department. Within twenty minutes Cyntal, surrounded by three tall firemen, was back in her apartment. The firemen had also rescued her dinner. When they left she threw the Macanudos in the trash.

One Word

By Linda Dogué Holliman

In one word

I can count the stars,

Splash in a tide pool,

Sing a melody,

And say

What you are to me.

Love.

I Remained Silent

By Grant Perryman

It has been said that a good story always starts at the beginning. In elementary school I was an avid reader. Reading was my escape from the turmoil of the 1960's. I could travel the world discovering mysterious places and incredible cultures. My favorite subject was history. I marveled at the ancients and their incredible wisdom. I realized future mistakes could be avoided if we learn from the past. The educational system at the time fell short when it came to American and World History. I was taught that Black History started with slavery and African History began with European colonization. I knew it was a lie and started to educate myself. By the time I was in ninth grade I had read every book in my local library and then some. In class we had an assignment to write about one of our ancestors who had immigrated from another country. I had to be excused from this assignment because I did not know. In frustration I went home and open my

1964 World Encyclopedia Set to a map of the continent of Africa.

I closed my eyes and was determined to "adopt" me a country. My finger landed on the West African country of Ghana. I was excited to learn more about its people, history, culture and traditions. I continued to vicariously travel through books to Ghana never thinking I could physically go there. My imagination was all I needed to be content.

Fast forward to 1999. My good friend and I wrote and directed an Easter play and held auditions for the theatrical production. After reading several lines, one particular individual was asked, as everyone else, if she would like to share a special talent or unique ability that would be useful for the play. Without hesitating she proceeded to do several back flips across the stage. After the applause subsided she explained she was a gymnastics coach at a local gym. Then Dawnita smiled and I was mesmerized.

Needless to say, Dawnita got the part and I quickly rewrote one scene for her character to be the girlfriend of my character. During our weekly rehearsals it became evident a love connection was blooming. It was evident to me because every time I was around her my hands began to sweat, I stuttered like a 3-year-old and I couldn't look her straight in her eyes. She had bewitched me with that smile. It was bedazzling. The play ran for three consecutive nights and everyone was pushing me to ask her out on a date. Lord knows I tried asking several times, but nothing came out of my mouth. I planned, I rehearsed yet nothing. Finally, on the last night after our couple scene, in sheer desperation I asked and she smiled.

Dawnita shared with me later on that after the first date she knew I was the one. So, after several dates she prayed according to Matthew 21:22 and asked God for a ring. A few months later, in December, it was her birthday and her parents gave her a birthstone ring. God answered her prayer, exactly. She laughed to herself and said, "God, you got jokes," realizing she did not ask specifically. So once again she prayed according to Matthew 7:7-11 and asked God for me to give her a ring.

We began rehearsal for a Christmas play that took place in modern times. She played a young lady of wealthy means. She told me she would just wear something out of her own closet as she could not afford to buy anything new for she was single and had to support her 5-year-old son. Well, on her birthday I presented to her a brand-new outfit and a beautiful costume ring. Again, God answered her prayer exactly. With a frustrated laugh and a lesson twice learned, she prayed one more time. "God, I would like a wedding ring from Grant."

Valentine's Day was approaching and it was on a Friday. Earlier in the week she asked if I had made any plans. I told her my church had a couples retreat to Yosemite on Saturday and I had paid for our seats. I said I would come over to her apartment after work on Friday and hang out for a few hours. I knew she would not expect me to propose to her on such an obvious occasion. So, I planned just that to surprise her.

After work I rushed home to get the ring, roses and card. I excitedly drove to her apartment and parked. Something was wrong. I didn't see her car. I knocked on her door. No answer. I called on the phone. No answer. I waited in my car. No Dawnita. I went home. The next day as we were on the bus going to Yosemite, she explained to me that she was called in to work unexpectedly and didn't think I would mind since our official date was on Saturday. I nodded and remained silent.

Every seven years my birthday falls on Mother's Day. By this time, Dawnita started attending my church with me and everyone loved her. I repeatedly asked what her plans were on Mother's Day which fell on a Sunday. She said she talked it over with her mom and that she would come to church with me and then would go visit her mom. I asked to be placed on the service program to make an announcement. It was my turn to prank my pastor. Let me explain. I was involved in a theatrical production outside of the church, which he attended and took great delight in the fact that my character was the devil.

I stood outside the front door awaiting Dawnita in the parking lot. I waited. I waited and waited. I went inside when the service began. I waited. I waited and waited. My time on the program was fast-approaching and I waited. I waited and waited, finally indicating to the announcer to cancel my time. That afternoon, I got a call from Dawnita explaining her mom had changed her mind and wanted her to come to church with her at the last minute. She asked me what she'd missed. With a frustrated laugh and a lesson twice learned, I planned one more time and I remained silent.

In the year 2000, a gentleman came from North Carolina to share his experience in Ghana, West Africa. He asked my pastor if he would come and commit our church for five years. Pastor Sam was Senior Pastor, Dean of Students at Bethany College and working on his Master's degree. He said he was too busy, but there was a guy in my congregation who thought he was African. I was not in the service at the time; I was helping set up our youth fundraiser. After service Pastor came to me and asked if I wanted to go to Ghana. My intelligent response was, "I don't have any money!"

"Boy, I didn't ask you that," was his reply. I was sent and instructed to bring back video to show the church and Board of Directors.

Dawnita's first mission trip to Ghana was in 2003. My pastor kept asking me in front of Dawnita when I was going to propose. I remained silent. Before we left for Ghana, Pastor Sam pulled me to the side and said, "Boy, I got you. You are going to propose in Africa. You the man!" I remained silent.

Our two-week mission trip went very well. The most incredible thing happened to Dawnita. Every day a local person would approach her speaking Twi, the Ashanti language. Others would say she was Ashanti based on her physical features.

Several times during our mission Pastor Sam would ask, "When are you going to propose?" To which, of course, I remained silent. Saturday afternoon, we were finishing a medical outreach in a rural community. I asked Dawnita to walk with me to watch the sunset by a nearby river. It was a beautiful scene with a gorgeous sunset. The soft breeze gently blew the trees. The birds were busily chatting away. Our eyes slowly meandered on each other's faces. She smiled. We were finally alone. I asked the question.

"Dawnita?"

"Yes?"

"Are you ready to leave? The bus is ready."

"Oh, okay."

This completed our mission trip and it was Sunday morning when I realized I had not thought about how I was going to propose. Back in the states I had asked Dawnita to help me make a banner with the name of Pastor Akumbie's church in Ghana which she would help me present to the congregation. I began to panic and quickly wrote a poem. Church service began and at the agreed upon time, Pastor Akumbie, who knew what was happening, called Dawnita and I for our "presentation." As we passed Pastor Sam, I heard him say, "I think he is going to do it."

I remained silent.

We presented the banner and after the thank yous and applause, Dawnita began walking back to her seat. I gently grabbed her hand and told her to stay. She gave me the most puzzled look. Through an interpreter, I explained to the congregation that she was my girlfriend, and to clear up confusion, she was American and not Ashanti. Tremendous applause came after the interpretation. Keeping my words in short phrases, I explained how much she meant to me. However, the more I talked the more nervous I became. My hands began to sweat and my face froze into a silly grin. I kept repeating the short poem I had composed to calm me down and then the thought, which hand and finger do I put the ring on, popped into my head. Now I was really nervous and felt like Niagara Falls was thundering down my face. The moment had arrived and I got down on one knee.

"Your eyes light up my life. Your laughter brings joy to my soul. Your smile calms the fears of my heart. You standing here next to me brings strength to my life. Please honor me today by becoming my wife."

Dawnita began to cry and shake but managed to extend the correct hand and finger. Pastor Samon and the front row were in tears. After service we went out for a late lunch and someone asked Dawnita what was her wedding dream. I thought she wanted the traditional Western wedding, with a white dress. She surprised me with her response, "I want an Ashanti wedding, and my future husband will plan it." Instantly, my mind went into creative planning mode.

I stayed another two weeks after the rest of the team left. I traveled to Kumasi and went to the village of Bonwire where the royal kente weavers reside. I picked out a traditional pattern called, "Ti koro nko agyina" meaning "Two heads are better than one."

The Ashanti people are ruled by a male and a female. The male, "Ashantihenne" or King of the Ashanti people and the female is "Ohemaa" or Queen

Mother who cannot be married to the king. The Ashanti people are matriarchal. The king's son does not become the next king. A son from a royal sister or aunt is nominated to become king by the Queen Mother. The Queen Mother has her own separate palace and court.

On festivals the feet of the Ashantihenne and Ohemaa are not allowed on the ground. They are carried in a palanquin under a large, colorful, bright umbrella. The palanquin is carried on the shoulders of male attendants. While in Kumasi I purchased an umbrella.

When I arrived back home I had my friend make a replica of the Queen Mother's chair palanquin. Dawnita and I picked a date but my future in-laws would be out of town. We picked another date and my parents would be out of town. We finally settled on March 6, 2014 which was Ghana's Independence Day. Throughout the process I shared most of my plans with Dawnita except her being carried down the aisle.

Two weeks before the wedding I stopped at our local library and heard drumming. I looked inside the room and I saw a woman dressed in the traditional clothes of Ghana teaching about her country's music and dances. I waited until the end and asked her if she could teach us the Adwoa dance for our wedding. She became excited when I told her about my plans. When I explained to her the secret of the chair palanquin, she burst laughing and said she would have to dance at my wedding.

March 6, 2014 arrived and it was a clear blue gorgeous day. The African drums began to play as

Pastor Akumbie came down the aisle with an opening prayer in the Twi language. Pastor Sam followed, translating into English. The wedding party marched in to "Mama Tembu is Getting Married", a popular South-African song. In Africa a wedding is not about two individuals getting married, it is about two families joining together. My entire family marched in with me to an Xhosa wedding song. My wife's family marched in to the roar of drums followed by the dancer from the library. Dawnita was carried down the aisle on her chair palanquin carried by four strong young men wearing Northern Ghanaian smocks. Above her twirled the royal umbrella held by her brother. It was a royal festive celebration. When we arrived at the altar my older brother began the "Knocking at the Door" ceremony. He asked if his family could pick a flower out of their garden. Usually it would take all day to negotiate the bride's price. When my in-laws accepted my brother clapped his hands and the four young men brought in four trunks containing clothing for my mother-in-law, cooking utensils for my wife, money, and since our families do not drink, sparkling apple cider.

For my wedding vows I commissioned a wooden plaque from Ghana with six carved "Adinkra" symbols. Adinkra means to say good-bye and they were traditionally used for funerals. There are hundreds of symbols, each with a proverb that is used every day. I read it aloud.

"God gave me you. A rare and precious gift of which there is no regret. Stamped in you is adinkrahene (that which stands out best and commands respect) because your faithfulness holds in every test. I promise to understand and love you with due respect til death ladder together we climb to rest."

My wife gave me a beautiful gold ring with the "Gye Nyame" adinkra symbol which translates "except God". At the end we danced the Adwoa dance to an Ashanti song underneath the royal umbrella and made the front page of our local Sunday newspaper, and I no long remained silent.

A Neighbor Moth
By Carl Weber

Coming home from work
I parked my bike on the porch
To find a neighbor moth
A prisoner of porch walls screened in.

My little moth just made bad choices
And didn't know where he was.
And now has learned some lessons
Trying to find the way out.

So in seeing it fly,
In panic and distress,
And wisdom less,
I guided its fright and flight
To a hole in the screen,
To see it return to a better world.

And now that the accident is over,
I turned to the door,
To go inside, thinking,
How much wisdom would it take to free me
And how long the moth had been there.

A Christmas Wish
By Steven R. Butler

The phone rang on that breezy overcast winter's day in December 1968. I was three months short of my 18th birthday.

"So the chains will fit?" I inquired of my boss, Alfred, from the local Chevron station.

"I have the charts right here in front of me, Steve," he responded. "The same chain size for both cars."

I thanked Al and hung up the phone. My last detail was confirmed; I could borrow the tire chains used on my friend's parents' 1966 Chevrolet for my '56 Ford, and I would be ready for my trip.

I had made one big Christmas wish that year: I would spend the best Christmas ever with my family in Weaverville. On that Sunday, December 22, I had spent the afternoon excitedly packing up my old Ford Fairlane for the four-hour trip from the Napa Valley to Trinity County. I had spent the last several weeks carefully choosing gifts for various family members.

The day before, I had borrowed the tire chains for what I dearly hoped would be a "White Christmas."

I reviewed my Christmas list. I had chosen a "Greatest Hits" album by the Association for my older sister Marilyn. A threefold wallet for Mom. My littlest brother Robert would turn 4 on his birthday in January. I couldn't wait to see his face when he opened his package with a new toy-logging truck. I had a carton of Pall Malls for Jimmie, and a book about baseball history for little brother Michael. And for Dad, I had done some projects in Metal Shop at St. Helena High. For his gift, I brought a couple of sizes of hand-forged cold chisels.

Sunday evening. I had everything in order. I had made this 250-mile trip to Trinity County numerous times in the past, mostly alone. The weather reports predicted a sizeable storm lurking from the Gulf of Alaska. But I was confident; I anticipated an enjoyable trip, one that I would remember for many years to come.

I finished my shift at the local Chevron station as usual at ten o'clock, and I started out over Mount St. Helena, and out through Lake County toward I5. True to prediction, the storm had moved in from the north, a steady rain had fallen for several hours.

The rain fell harder as I followed Highway 20 across into the Sacramento Valley. Dave Diamond's show on KFRC radio had gone off, and night jockey Bo Weaver had taken over the airwaves at midnight. Around 12:30am, I drove into an all-night Chevron just outside of Williams.

"Where ya headed?" the twenty-something gas jockey inquired as he collected my money for 12 gallons of regular.

"Trinity County," I spoke proudly. "Gonna spend the week up there. Family lives outside Weaverville." He looked out the window of the station. The canopy lights illuminated the steady rain that splattered down onto the dark tarmac.

"I'd take somethin' hot if I was you; some coffee, or hot chocolate. And something to eat, too. A chocolate bar or two. You don't want to get stuck up there on Buckhorn without nothing to eat."

I took his advice. Couple of Almond Joy bars. A cup of hot chocolate. A pack of Marlboros. I wondered why I had not thought of snacks when I left home. No big deal. I hit the road again.

The rain continued to fall at a vigorous pace as I rolled past the little town of Willows. I cruised along the deserted stretch of I5 at a smooth 65 mph, my 292 Thunderbird V8 singing its soothing rumbling song. Rock and roll from a Sacramento station crackled through the tinny stock speakers on the AM radio.

A few miles south of Orland, the rain increased and the wind picked up. I stepped the windshield wipers to full speed. I held my pace. Just a few other cars shared that stretch of freeway.

Suddenly the rain began to transform, turning quickly to slush. My windshield wipers at full speed could barely keep the windshield clear. Next, I felt as though I had gone from one room into another, from a dark rainy night to a glistening sea of white. The rain turned to snow; moments earlier I had sailed along smoothly at 65 miles per hour. I bogged down to under 35, slogging my way through a heavy blanket of freshly fallen snow.

Just up the freeway, I could see the illumination of an overhead light at the next off-ramp. I mushed toward the ramp and exited the freeway. At the end of the off-ramp, I stepped hard on the brake pedal to stop. My old Ford kept going, sliding neatly through the stop sign, ending up sideways in the middle of County Road 27.

"Great," I thought. "Time for the chains." I opened the door and stepped out into the night under the yellowish glow of the street light. My foot sunk deep into the fresh powder. I looked around in awe, looking up into the glow of the overhead light, watching as the falling snowflakes glistened in the cold winter air.

The overhead light was not enough to see to mount the tire chains. My car sat in at least a foot of fresh powder. I would have needed to shovel it away to clear the way to mount the chains. I needed a gas station or an open lot with some light.

Back out on the deserted freeway, a Peterbilt tractor and semi-trailer sloshed past at about 40 miles per hour. I knew I would have to make do, maybe all the way to Redding. Another hour, at least. But if I stayed close to the big Pete, at least he could clear a trail ahead of me. I got back into the car and headed back to the freeway.

Most all radio reception had faded out by now, as I caught a funky detective show broadcast from an all-night station in Salt Lake City. I accelerated to speed, but I realized that at any speed over 35, my car's rear end would slip and slide precariously, so I held that pace. Very little heat flowed through my heater or defroster ducts, so the wipers struggled to clear half-frozen snow from my windshield. The darkness seemed to get even darker. The car's cabin chilled.

"Take some hot coffee," I recalled the words of the gas station attendant. My chocolate was gone. And even on that familiar stretch of I5, I felt lost. Everywhere I looked, I saw nothing but a blanket of dark white snow. Tire tracks cut through the soft snow by the big Peterbilt became my only means of navigation, my only sense of direction between the lights over the overpasses.

In the distance I could still see the Big Pete. I pushed the gas pedal, hoping to at least keep the taillights in view. In the heavy snow, I could see just a short distance ahead of me. But the taillights faded ahead and finally disappeared.

I didn't know the time when I rolled into Redding. At an all-night truck stop off Highway 273, I drove up to a fairly clear spot at the outside pump block. I knew I could use some gas. But most importantly, I needed to put on my chains. I had managed to buck through the snow on I5, but I would have no chance against the conditions on 299 over Buckhorn Summit.

"Hey, how's it goin'?" a chubby fiftyish-looking gas attendant quipped as he greeted me.

"Hi," I returned. "Could you fill it with regular? And do you mind if I use your pump block? I need to put my chains on."

"I'spose not," he answered reluctantly. I'd probably been his only customer in the last hour or better, so I didn't think that my using his pump block would cause much delay for anyone.

He proceeded to fill the gas tank. I went to work on the chains. I jacked up the car. The right chain went on smoothly. The left chain wasn't so cooperative. I got the inside latch fastened, but the outside latch fell about an inch short of closing.

"Damn!" I thought. What rotten luck. My boss at the Chevron, Al had assured me that these chains would fit my tire size perfectly. I continued to struggle with the chain. After a half-hour or so, the gas jockey came over to see why I was taking so long with the chains.

"I can't get it latched," I sighed.

"You got the right chains?"

"Yeah, I'm sure I do. The other one went on fine."

"Sometimes the tread depth varies. You got the same tires on here?"

He took a look. He mumbled to himself.

"Just a minute." He went to the lube room and brought out a pair of pliers and some bailing wire.

"You might try this. At least you can get it to stay 'til you get where you're going." I agreed, and I wrapped a couple of loops of wire and managed to hook the chain.

"Where are you going anyhow?" he asked.

"Over Buckhorn to Weaverville," I answered.

"I'd wait'll tomorrow if I was you," he warned. "You don't wanna get stuck up there."

"Thanks," I responded. "And thanks for the wire. I appreciate your help." I got back into the car and started out toward 299 west.

I continued up 273 to 299, the chains thumping as I accelerated, and then smoothing out to a steady drone against the pavement as I maintained a steady 30 miles per hour. I made the turn west onto Highway 299 toward Weaverville. With the chains on, I felt much more secure. I had traction so I knew I had at a least chance to keep from getting stuck in a snow drift. But the wired chain continued to haunt me. What if the bailing wire broke? The chain would wrap around the brake line and rip it loose, spewing brake fluid everywhere. My brakes would be gone. And so would one chain. I would be marooned.

My radio station had faded out. I felt painfully alone. The radio crackled with static, with very few clear signals from anywhere across the dial. I gave up and turned it off. I drew my wool jacket around my neck to stay warm.

I drove through the little town of Mount Shasta, past Whiskeytown Lake, and past the turnoff for French Gulch. The roadway got darker, flanked only by the reflective white mileage markers and a series of tracks made by previous travelers.

The road ahead of me seemed to remind me of my own life. A dark winding road that seemed to vanish into a very dark future.

My mind continued to drift. A Beach Boys' car song echoed monotonously in my head as my thoughts scrolled through memories of life at home in Weaverville. On a snowy or rainy day, we kids would entertain ourselves with pencils and pads, with records and a small battery- powered turn table.

I continued west on 299. The snow continued to fall and the visibility had become even worse. I not only lost track of the time, but I also lost track of my whereabouts. The snowplow had gone through on 299 earlier, but another hour of snowfall had left a coat of white over the entire road, and I could barely see the tracks of earlier travelers.

I reached the 2000-foot elevation mark. I pushed on, trying vainly to identify landmarks. The terrain got steeper as I slowly climbed toward the summit. The curves got tighter, and I felt my car slipping as I pressed through the steeper turns.

I reached the 3000-foot elevation sign. Feeling a bit of relief, I knew I only had a few more miles to the summit. My chains droned against the pavement as I wound my way up the mountain grade. I reached the 4000-foot level. The road straightened out and I accelerated past the summit sign, and started down the other side. I had completed one major leg of the trip. I realized that I hadn't passed a single other car since before Whiskeytown Lake.

The snowfall lightened after I crested the summit. I passed the snow plow just before the Lewiston turnoff. The heavy veil of the storm had lifted; I could see enough to identify my location. I cruised down the mountain past Fawn Lodge, along the Trinity River into Douglas City, and I continued west on 299. I reached what should have been my destination, Little Brown's Creek Road. I stopped just before the bridge, eased to a stop, and looked at the sight.

The snow plows had opened enough of the highway for two clear lanes of traffic. But the plows had piled a drift of snow at least ten feet deep across the end of Little Brown's Creek Road. How would I get through that? And I had nowhere to park either. But I would have to deal with that detail later. Right now, I sat somewhere between midnight and nowhere; I would need some daylight. I needed a different plan.

I resumed driving, continuing west along Highway 299 toward Weaverville. I recalled, our neighbors from Brown's Mountain, the Martins, had moved into town the previous fall. I could go to their house. At least I would have somewhere to stop. To think. To plan. Then, after daylight, I could face the huge snow drift.

I found the town of Weaverville blacked out from one end to the other. Not a single streetlight glowed in the snowy winter terrain. My headlights cut through the dark town as I cruised past the darkened buildings, past the spiral staircases in front of the historic hotels on Main Street, past the post office, and the court house, to the turnoff to Hanley's Lumber Yard. I eased off Main Street onto the side street that led up a hill to a row of small cottages.

I eased my way up the narrow road. Which cottage? The darkness didn't help with my navigation. And every light was out, leaving me with just my headlights to try to identify the Martins' cottage.

The snow plow hadn't cleared the road. I mushed my way slowly up the hill in the darkness. I got as far as I could before deciding to retreat back toward a clearer space. I shifted into reverse, trying to back down the hill. The rear of my car slipped to the left, giving way. I slid backward into what felt like a ditch.

"Damn!" I shifted into drive and accelerated, but I had slipped too far. My wheels spun in the snow. I was stuck. I shut off the engine.

What could I do? I couldn't tell the time, but it was way too early to call on John and Evelyn. My car was not going anywhere.

So, I stretched out on the front seat and tried to sleep.

I awoke some time later. I didn't know how long I had slept, but I knew I hadn't rested. I stirred my stiff frame to life and sat up on the passenger's side of the front seat. The daylight had broken, and the snow had stopped, but the gray hazy fog hung over the cold morning, cutting visibility down to just a stone's throw or less.

I pulled my jacket around my stiff, chilled body. Ah, that hot cup of coffee. Of course, it would have been cold coffee by now. I pulled the door handle and pushed the door open, and stepping out into the freshly fallen snow, I saw that I had backed down the narrow street and slipped into a small ditch. One rear wheel on my car hung there in a drift of snow.

"Oh, great," I thought. "Now, how the hell am I going to get out of there?"

I looked back up the road to where I thought I remembered the Martins' cottage. Would I be lucky and find them home? A white Volkswagen Beetle sat in front of the cottage. Where was the Chevy panel truck? Or the Cadillac?

"One way to find out," I thought. And at that time I could think of nothing more desirable than a hot cup of coffee and some breakfast.

I walked up the hill and knocked on the door. Something felt amiss. An older man, fiftyish, medium-build with silvery brown hair answered the door.

"Hi," I greeted.

"Hello, greetings to you," he said with a smile.

"Um," I felt dumbfounded.

"Can I help you?"

"Uh, yeah," I stammered. "I was looking for John and Evelyn Martin."

"Nobody here by that name, sorry."

I just stood there. I didn't know what to say. Now what would I do? My car was stuck. I had no way to get home. I was lost.

"They lived here last summer," I continued. "In this house."

"I moved here last month."

"Oh, okay," I muttered weakly. "So, I guess they moved." I turned to leave. "Sorry to bother you."

"Hey, you look like you could use some coffee," he spoke up. I turned back and smiled. "Come on in."

"Thanks, man," I responded. I stepped into the warmth of the small cottage.

"So, where ya from?" he asked.

"Saint Helena," I responded. "In the Napa Valley."

We introduced ourselves. He said his name. Arthur. I didn't catch his last name.

He poured two cups of hot coffee. We sipped our coffee and chatted.

"I came here in October for a logging job," he explained. "Worked for a couple months or so in Junction City. Been living here since. Prob'ly move back to Marysville in another few weeks. Sorry, I don't know about your friends."

"I came over Buckhorn Summit last night. On my way home for Christmas. Headed for Little Brown's Creek."

"My Volksie wouldn't be much help for your Ford, I'm afraid," he said. "But I know who could help. Soon as we get some coffee down our necks, I'll give you a lift down to Raley's. He's got a tow rig that'll get you on the road in no time. And we can stop down at Katie's. I'll bet you could go for a plate of eggs and hash browns."

"Yes, sir," I agreed. "I think you're playin' my song."

We had breakfast at the little coffee shop on Main Street near Trinity High. Then he drove me up the street to Raley's Chevron.

"Say, my friend here could use a hand," Arthur beckoned as we pulled up to the pump block at the Main Street station. "He got his car buried in a drift up my way."

"Stuck in the snow, eh?" Rex Raley sneered. I could sense what he was thinking, wondering what the hell I was doing out in a storm like this one.

"Just came over Buckhorn last night," I stated soberly. "I need to get home. Out to Little Brown's Creek."

"What's your name, son?"

"Steve Butler," I responded.

"Came over Buckhorn? Last night? Whoa, what a trip that must've been."

I nodded. His stern look softened, melting into a smile.

"Say...you're Bob Butler's son, aren't you?"

"Yes, sir," I answered. "I know your son, Terry."

"Well, don't worry." He smiled. "We'll get you home. Just give me another ten minutes or so, and I'll get the tow rig out."

Within a half-hour, we got my car out of the snowbound ditch. I paid Mr. Raley for the tow. Five bucks for a twenty-dollar tow. I thanked him. He wished me well.

Then I thanked Arthur for all of his help.

"My pleasure," he smiled. We shared a handshake. "Good luck on your trip home. And I hope you find your friends, the Martins."

I felt fortunate. But the toughest leg of the trip, I suspected, was yet to come. Driving out to the turnoff for Little Brown's Creek took a mere ten minutes. But now I faced a mountain of snow that had increased significantly since I drove past it only hours before.

I looked around, but I could see nowhere that I could park off the road. I turned the car around as though I was headed back to Weaverville. As I did, I noticed a slight notch in the pile of snow, possibly wide enough that I could squeeze my car off the road far enough to park. I nosed the car into the small space. I looked around. Not far enough. The back bumper still stuck out too far. I pulled the gear shift into low range, and planted the front wheel against the edge of the large mound of snow. I accelerated hard. The right front fender dozed into the piled snow. I stopped and shut off the engine.

I got out and looked round. I had two wheels up on the snow drift and two on the pavement. The right side of my car sat pressed against a wall of snow. Close enough. I was far enough off the road that traffic could pass. Hopefully I wouldn't have to leave the car there very long.

I pulled a sweatshirt on over my shirt and my jacket over it. Then I set out for my two-mile hike for home. I waded through the deep drift, thoroughly soaking my jeans from the thighs down. Past the drift built up by the snow plow, the fresh snow lay over knee-deep. Fresh powder slipped into my tall rubber boots with each and every step. I slogged up the slope, through the narrows to the fork in the road.

I thought of all the days that I had walked this road from the bus stop after school. I walked past the blind curve, past the first cabin, and up through the big hook curve. I reached the Shabers' house. It sat silently off to the right of the roadway.

I couldn't feel my toes in my soaked boots. The deep snow on the open areas of the road lay about two-feet deep, and made walking difficult. The snow in the areas shielded by trees was shallower, where could I walk without a struggle. I pushed on. I couldn't be more than a half-hour from home.

I continued up the straightaway past the second cabin. My spirits lifted as I humped up the last hill before the bridge. I saw the high voltage power lines in the distance, the "warning track," as I used to call them, an indication that I was almost home. I crossed the old log bridge below the house across Little Brown's Creek and headed up the hill. I could see the house. I stopped briefly to take in the sight.

I heard the roar of an engine, and I looked ahead to see Dad with our old Ford tractor on the upper flat next to the road, clearing snow, as Jimmie and my little brother Robert looked on. I watched as he made repeated passes with the box scraper, pulling all the way forward and then backing hard against a huge pile of snow, pushing it down over the bank to the creek.

He saw me and stopped. At first, he could not believe his eyes. He shut down and climbed off the tractor.

"Hey, how'd you get here?" he asked, bewildered. "Where's your car?"

"A long story. Car's at the end of the road," I responded. I was too exhausted to explain. He reached for me and we shared a greeting handshake.

"Yeah, I came over the mountain last night." He just smiled, shaking his head.

"Well, welcome home," he said. "You'd better get your butt in there in front of that stove. Get out of those wet clothes. And have your mother get you some coffee."

I smiled with relief. As I headed down the path to the house, my little brother following in my footsteps, my eyes felt misty; I wasn't sure whether from the fog hanging over the canyon or the joy of being home.

The week went way too fast. On Thursday, the day after Christmas, the road grader rumbled up Little Brown's Creek Road, clearing the snow from the old country road. On Friday, December 27th, I loaded up my old Ford and bid good-bye to my family, ready to make the four-hour trip back to St. Helena, my job, and St. Helena High School

At the end of the road, at Highway 299, as I stopped to shed my car's tire chains, I paused. I pictured little brother Robert out in the yard with his logging truck, Mom with her new wallet, Marilyn listening to the sounds of the Association on our old battery turntable, Mike reading his baseball history and dreaming of playing ball, little sister Carol enjoying her books and Jimmie sitting at the dining room table enjoying another Pall Mall.

The trip home would be comparably routine. But little did I realize, the memory of this Christmas, already emblazoned in my mind, would remain a fond memory for years to come.

The Best You Can Do Always Matters

Vicki Ward

Nia walked slowly down the street, deep in thought, Rashan's words replaying in her mind. Deep in thought without looking, she stepped off the sidewalk into the street. She didn't see the car approaching fast around the corner. Suddenly, she heard tires squealing as the car skidded to avoid hitting her. She screamed, quickly backing up, landing flat on her back in the grass of a nearby house.

A little dazed she looked around and saw the car resting against the curb across the street with the motor running, and the driver glaring at her. Instantly angered by his scowling face, she jumped to her feet and in seconds was at the driver's door.

"What's wrong with you speeding down the street like a maniac? You could have killed me," she screamed, her face contorted with anger, arms flailing.

She was so angry she didn't notice a figure had gotten out from the passenger side of the car and was now just steps from her. She felt his presence, turning abruptly and was face-to-face with a tall dark-skinned man. He was walking up to her with his hands up, like he was about to surrender, but also ready to deflect what may have been an angry swing in his direction.

"Hold it, hold it, just calm down," he said.

Nia looked up at him and back to the driver who hadn't moved, nor had he changed his expression, which made her anger throttle up more.

"What do you want?" she hissed.

"I'm trying to see if you're okay. Are you all right?" the passenger asked a little firmer, trying to get her to calm down.

"I'm fine, no thanks to you two. What do you want?"

"I know you almost got hit and I just want to see if you're okay."

Nia looked hard at his face. His didn't have the scowl that the driver's face held. She felt the panic, and fear receding a little.

"Yeah, I'm fine, but why the hell was he driving so fast? And why's he looking at me like I was the one speeding down the street?" she quickly rattled off.

"I can't answer that, I'm just glad you're all right."

"Why? So I won't call the police on his sorry ass? You probably wouldn't like it too much if I called the police, would you?" she shouted in the driver's direction.

The driver quietly cursed as he threw his head back. The passenger looked at him, then back to Nia. His face softened and he straightened his back, lowering his hands before speaking.

"Look, I'm sorry you were almost hurt. I can take you anywhere you need to go."

"You think I'm gonna get into that car with you and him? Then you're really stupid," she said as her anger began to rise again.

"No, I didn't mean anything by that. I just thought you might need a ride, that's all. Here, let me write down my phone number and if you're hurt you can let me know, okay?"

Nia was quietly seething. He held out a small piece of paper to her. She looked at him coolly. "I can take care of myself, but if I need to go to the hospital you're gonna pay for it," she snapped and snatched the paper from his hand, turned and walked away.

Her head was really banging now; on top of everything happening with Rashan, she had this near-accident to deal with too. She was almost at the BART Station and what was supposed to be a short walk to clear her head did the opposite. She glanced at her watch and knew she missed her regular train and would have to stand all the way home.

Once she arrived at the station she reached for her ticket, but it wasn't in the side zipper section of her backpack where she always kept it. She sighed heavily and moved away from the entry gates, as she knew not to delay the crush of workers, and students heading home. Experience taught her commuters would trample anyone who stood in the way of them boarding a train. She searched her pockets, and then stopped suddenly, her mind going back to the near- accident.

"Oh no," she stated loudly.

Those walking near her gave odd glances as they quickly moved to another line of the pay gates. She remembered what happened. She had taken the transit pass out of her backpack and had it in her hand walking down the street. When she got up from the ground she made sure she wasn't hurt, and that her backpack was secure, but never thought about the transit pass.

"Damn," she said aloud.

Her heart sank, remembering the ticket was nearly new, with almost $40.00 on it, and because she had to stop to purchase another ticket, might miss catching the next train. By now she was feeling doubly deflated, just limp. She was all out of fight and about ready to cry. She shut out thoughts, purchased a ticket, went through the pay gate and up the escalator. She lifted her head only slightly to make sure she was headed toward the right platform.

Looking up she stared at the people, and billboards, trying not to think of anything else, but that didn't last. She was silently cursing that ugly fool for nearly running her down, and to top it off he caused her to lose nearly $40.00. She wanted to slap the hell out of him, wished she had done it when she was standing by his car. All she could think of was that scowl he had on his face, like she was the one doing *him* wrong.

Nia knew she wouldn't find a seat and once on the train didn't try. She settled in next to the door, grabbed the nearest pole and just let the rhythm of the speeding car take her physically and mentally away. She watched the landscape and the familiar look of the city change to the sprawl of the suburbs as the train rushed further away from the city.

Finally, her stop was approaching. She looked up or opened an eye occasionally to determine just where on the homebound journey she was; it only took one time to sleep past her stop, and vowed it would never happen again.

Nia spent much of the evening wrestling with thoughts about her conversation with Rashan, and that stupid driver and the near-miss getting killed on the street that followed on her way to catch her train home.

Rashan always had a gift for the dramatic, and never met a crisis he could not exaggerate, to make himself look better. Their relationship had begun and endured for a little over one year. The beginning was slow and casual. They actually met on the train. During her trips to work in the morning, and home again at the end of the day, they had seen each other from time to time. Occasionally, their eyes met; each nodded acknowledging the other, yet they never spoke or had any contact.

One day while she was commuting to work, he got on the train as usual. She was reading and didn't look up, or notice him until he eased into the empty seat next to her. She was a bit startled, and almost flustered, as they spoke for the first time. Their introductions encouraged friendly talk and continued until she reached her stop. They began to share conversation often during their commute.

They learned both were single, and found they enjoyed some of the same things, music, movies, and weekend fun. They began dating and several months later, they were seeing each other often. Thinking back to how they had evolved, made Nia angrier, because they agreed to be straight if things changed, or if either one became dissatisfied with the relationship.

Well, he broke the rule and decided to test the water with someone different and now had a baby on the way with someone he thought would only be a *short stop* for him. She had to shut down her thoughts. It was just too much to process.

The following evening, she had to blink several times to make sure she was not having a flash of anger, because standing directly in front of her near the entrance to the BART Station was a figure she instantly recognized. Standing there with a smile on his face looking at her was the passenger from the car that almost killed her yesterday. Recognition and anger surged in her quickly.

"What are you doing here? Are you stalking me? she hissed through tightly clenched lips, quickly trying to get past him to the entrance gate.

"Now hold up just a minute." I came here to give you something you lost and thought if I came to this station at the same time of day I might find you to give you this." He reached into his pocket and held a Bart Ticket close to her face. Nia stopped suddenly, her eyes locked on the ticket.

"Where did you get that?"

"You must have dropped this yesterday when you fell."

"You mean when I was nearly run down and fell into that yard."

"Look, I'm not here to debate that again. I know how frightening that was, and just feel bad that you had to go through that. You had every right to be angry; I want to apologize again for the driver."

"It should be him standing here with an apology," she sniped.

"I know, but I was determined to find you, apologize and return this to you. I found it on the ground near where you fell and wanted to get it back to you. Don't worry, you won't see me again. I was taught that doing the best you can do always matters, and that's the only thing I am here to do."

He turned and walked away as she stood there looking confused but appreciated his honesty and the gesture he made to find her.

Later that week, she reconciled the dilemma Rashan had created. Though they had more than just a casual relationship, she decided to remove herself from discussions, deleting distracting, emotional drama and protecting her emotions, to allow him to deal with his issues.

Remembering what the passenger in the car that almost hit her said, reminded her, about how doing the best you can always mattered, and took his advice. Rashan needed time to do the best he could, which mattered most at this point and she didn't want to be a factor in the decision nor have a coronary over the process.

An Excerpt from The Duke

By Alan Werblin

I feel the need to tell my father's story, since he never would have thought to tell it himself. He was born in 1916, into the proverbial lap of luxury: a "seven-month baby", one kilo (2.2 pounds) at birth, no longer than a bread knife. His father, Abner, had to carry him in a shoebox filled with olive oil-soaked cotton to a nearby hospital that had an incubator. He still was not expected to survive. A relative passing Abner in the hall, peeked into the box and commented, "Hardly worth saving!" But survive he did, into life on Park Avenue with a chauffeur, a German governess, and world-travelling parents.

My father, Mayer Monroe Werblin, was the second-born child and first-born son of Abner Schuyler Werblin and Cecile Fellerman Werblin, Jewish immigrants who had prospered in the New York City of the early twentieth century.

My grandfather, Abner, or Poppa as I knew him, arrived at Ellis Island from Belarus at the age of four with his parents and four older sisters. Soon he was selling newspapers, and learning English well enough to put himself through night law school at CCNY, by teaching English as a second language.

Before long he was speculating on the roller coaster called Wall Street: buying and selling highly volatile securities, and amassing a sizeable nest egg. He took his money, and boarded a train to Shreveport, Louisiana where he purchased a horse, and rode around the countryside purchasing mineral and oil drilling rights from local farmers. On his return to NYC, he sold the rights and invested the money into margin stock purchases worth millions.

As their lifestyle prospered, my grandparents travelled the world: cruising to Europe, Asia and Africa, often leaving my dad and his older sister Florice in the care of governesses, house staff and extended family. Florice inhabited her own world, emotionally and intellectually hindered. It is unclear exactly to what extent because things like that were not discussed in those days.

When my father turned thirteen, his parents enrolled him at Valley Forge Military Academy in Pennsylvania. He would remain there until graduation six years later, except for infrequent visits home, learning manners, rifle and parade technique, discipline, and cavalry skills. His classmate, J.D. Salinger ran away, never to return.

While my father was away at school, the New York Stock Exchange crashed and stocks that were bought on margin were "called in". Those, like my grandfather, who were unable to cover their investments with liquid assets lost the value of their purchases. My family thus suffered a devastating financial loss, and although they were able to maintain appearances, their status and free-spending lifestyle was restricted.

On graduation from Valley Forge, my father was required to seek work, attend school and make his way in the world. Initially, he was enrolled at West Point, but was unable to attend. He then attempted to attend Johns Hopkins University to study medicine but was unable to muster the finances. He worked at various jobs, attended NYU School of Commerce and ran with a fast crowd of wealthy youngsters.

Meanwhile, my grandfather had reinvented himself as the owner of a business press that primarily printed glossy prospecti and annual reports. My grandmother, Cecile, was stricken with cancer and was chronically ill and bed-bound for the remainder of her life.

My dad and a friend, moved to Puerto Rico, where he ran a military clothing store. My dad had not qualified for military service due to stomach ulcers, which troubled him his entire life. Dad assimilated into the Puerto Rican lifestyle learning Spanish, dating Puerto Rican women, and adopting a more pronounceable name, Duke Warner.

One particular girl he dated for a number of months until she took him home to meet her parents. He saw an elderly dark-skinned woman sitting on the porch and when he inquired who she was the girl said, "my grandmother". Due to this revelation, he stopped seeing her. In later years dad candidly admitted this.

When he returned home, partially due to his mother's declining health, Dad met a young woman to whom he had been introduced by his father. Mimi Hostin, a petite singer who performed with big bands and on radio shows, and worked as a secretary in a raincoat establishment where Poppa chanced to buy a raincoat. Poppa introduced her to my dad and in 1943 they were married at my grandmother's bedside. She passed away 10 days later. The couple then moved to Columbus, Georgia, where my father ran a clothing store at Fort Benning's Post Exchange.

My parents stayed about a year in Georgia; due to my mother's homesickness and the oppressive anti-Semitism they faced. Jews were still considered as Christ killers, drinkers of children's blood. My father encountered signs at businesses that warned, "NO NIGGERS or JEWS ALLOWED."

Back in NYC, they moved into an apartment in the same building as Jenny Hostin, my mom's mother. It was on 95th Street and Riverside Drive, near Riverside Park and within walking distance of Broadway and its melting pot of Jews, African Americans, Puerto Ricans, Italians and a potpourri of fruit markets, butcher shops, laundries and other small businesses.

My father was able to find a job in a buying office, ordering men's clothing from manufacturers to be sold in department stores. This became his career for the next 40 years. Along the way, despite the high percentage of Jews in this industry, he lost more than one job due to his Jewish ethnicity, even being told,

"I'd love to hire you, Monroe, you're one of the 'good Jews'." Monroe turned this offer down.

By this time Abner had remarried to Gertrude, a much younger divorcee, with whom he continued his world travels and exorbitant lifestyle. Florice had married a non-Jew and was living in squalid conditions in Brooklyn with her husband, Mike. The family rarely visited them, but Abner helped support the couple. Mimi's brother Milton lived in Forest Hills, Queens with his wife, Muriel.

After eight years of marriage, in 1951, I was born and we continued to live in the apartment on Riverside Drive. Mimi pushed me in a carriage up to Broadway to shop or to Riverside Park to play and socialize. With a baby living with them in the apartment and Mimi's mother living upstairs, things got somewhat claustrophobic for the Werblins, especially for Dad. In addition, the neighborhood was "changing" and suburban sprawl was beckoning with its tidy little Cape Cod homes, bus lines which took you into the heart of Manhattan in thirty minutes, cheap mortgages and secret covenants banning people of color.

In 1954 we moved to Teaneck, New Jersey. Dad would take the bus daily to the Port Authority Bus Terminal in Manhattan and walk to work. My grandmother could come visit, and the growing family had a yard and two bedrooms on a quiet, tree-lined street. In 1955 my sister, Cele, was born.

My parents put me in daycare for the first time during my mom's hospital stay and were shocked when they received a call that I was crying hysterically to see my Uncle Arthur. They responded that I didn't have an Uncle Arthur, but later found out it was a kiddies' show I had been accustomed to watching on television.

In 1956, I started kindergarten at Longfellow Elementary. My first three years in school were difficult with anxiety demonstrated by daily episodes of nausea and occasional vomiting. Mimi said the school janitor was my best friend. Our car pool mates were not. Dad continued to gain confidence in his field and by all appearances experienced domestic bliss. Although, he shocked me many years later when he confessed to having had an affair with our neighbor Lucille, unbeknownst to my mother and Lucille's husband, Linwood.

One evening, in 1959, Mimi's mother, Jennie, was visiting us and woke up with chest pain and passed away en route to the doctor's office. My father delivered the news to me while I was sitting on his lap and broke down crying as he told me. Mimi became despondent and lonely and soon the family decided to move from the house in Teaneck. Mimi said she could no longer tolerate living in the house where her mother had died. They had a big split-level home built in Oradell, NJ, and moved.

In the fall, I started 3rd grade at Oradell Public School. My father continued to commute to NYC by bus. Mimi joined Jewish civic organizations such as O.R.T. (Organization for Rehabilitation through Training), started playing in a weekly Mah Jong game, and indulged in a nightly glass of gin or scotch. She also began dying her hair red, just like her mother. For Dad, being in the police reserves was a return to the discipline, uniforms and practice range he had experienced at Valley Forge. He would help direct traffic at civic events, parades, holidays, etc. We were proud of him: sharp in his uniform and cap. In addition, he had an abiding love of nature and the outdoors. He loved identifying plants and wildlife. My grandfather had a summer house in upstate New York with two ponds and woods surrounding. My father would take me on nature hikes and point out all the local trees and plants. He once shot a muskrat from the porch of the house that was submerged in the pond. He also disposed of baby skunks and shot a four-foot rattlesnake.

Family discipline was usually administered by Dad: reluctantly so. He was able to do it in a reserved manner; in contrast to my mother's lightning attacks: fueled by anger. He had a wooden bolo paddle, the type that had a red rubber ball attached by a thin elastic cord. He removed the cord and ball and *Voila!* He had a *bonafide* spanking tool. I later convinced him that the staple that remained was cruel and unusual punishment; and he agreed to remove that as well. Spankings were administered in my parents' bedroom and often were preceded by pleading, negotiations and requests for pre-administration demonstrations. "Show me first how hard you're going to hit me."

His reply was always, "This is going to hurt me more than it hurts you." I believed him.

I was directly affected and influenced by my father's career in the menswear industry. I rarely had to buy clothes as he was richly supplied with samples from boys and men's manufacturers, which I wore to school. I always had the latest fashions, even if I received them before my fellow students were aware they were fashionable. My father was always dressed impeccably and conservatively and had a closet and bureau that were neatly organized and color and seasonally coordinated. I also attended quarterly men's sportswear shows with him where a young boy could meet local sports figures, get autographs and receive personalized giveaways from the clothing companies displaying their lines for the upcoming season. My dad also passed on his immense knowledge of men's' clothing to me and taught me how to dress properly—how to tie a tie, how to distinguish a sports coat from a suit jacket, a dress shirt from a sports shirt; how to match colors and patterns, how long pants should be, what button to button, etc. etc. etc. These are knowledge and skills that I use every day and have taught my son and many others.

I was always mystified when my dad would know that I'd been "snooping" in his closet or drawers, believing that I restored everything just as I'd found it, but dad was as meticulous and neat as they come and he'd always notice I'd been there. When I discovered his stash of *Playboy* magazines in his closet, I believed I was really in trouble but he agreed to let me look at them so I would see they were not "dirty" or "forbidden fruit". That went a long way toward decreasing my desire to look at them and increasing my status with friends.

Campus Cacophony
By Linda Dogue' Holliman

A locomotive's lonely air horn moans, then the
    mile-long freight train barrels through;
wheels screech and railcars rattle, as the crossing
    gate bell clangs.
Streetcars whir along gleaming light rail tracks.
Shuttle busses huff and hiss at each stop.
Maintenance and delivery trucks beep in reverse
    and honk forward.

Two fire engines zoom; their sirens blare.
An ambulance screams into the teaching
    hospital's emergency entrance driveway.
A police car whoop whoops in flashes of red at
    the one who just slid through a four-way stop
    sign. Oops!

A student's inherited family car barely fires up
    then fputs. Oh, oh, try again.
Shiny steel-mobiles thump and bump vibrations of
    rap and rock.
A car alarm cannot be silenced.
Tires squeal on the turns of a parking structure
    just before the exit gate buzzer warns
    inattentive sidewalk pedestrians of an
    exiting vehicle.

Cell phones ring; elevators ding.
Skateboards kerplunk kerplunk on sidewalk
    cracks and suddenly scrape to a stop.
Chains clack and brakes squeak on dozens of
    sun-faded bicycles, soon overtaken by the racy
    purr of sleek road bikes whizzing by.
A solitary Segway balance scooter whirs smoothly
    along a tree shaded pathway.

The thud-ping of a pile driver echoes through the
    endowment-financed construction site of the
    new science hall.
Massive cooling units hiss and drip in the hot sun.
The campus bell tower bongs.
The student union PA system pumps out
    hip-shaking tunes that dance above the
    center's open air walkways.
An unidentifiable clamor pours out from a
    geometric arrangement of expressively
    decorated dorm windows.

The marching band drumline clatters a cadence
   on the distant practice field.
A neighborhood church bell welcomes weekday
   worshipers.
Military jets roar overhead at an acute angle.

How can any studying get done?

For the Love of Family
By Naomi Connor

After hand-washing the second load of dishes, Mia took a paper towel, splashed it with a little ammonia and proceeded to make a circular motion on the kitchen window. She always enjoyed a view of the outdoors. The blue sky, soft, billowy clouds, the blooming flowers being invaded by humming birds flitting about. It was an outdoor concert. An artist's perception of beauty in motion.

Another Saturday morning and the family was just about to do the weekend dance from the refrigerator to the breakfast counter. As soon as the meal was prepared, it was devoured. The clinking sound of silverware against stoneware; a culinary symphony. Truly another example of nature in motion.

The smiles and thoughtfulness in thanking their mother for her efforts had been part of lessons learned from early childhood. Be courteous, thankful and kind; a motto that this family put into practice. These were all attributes that Mia took pride in when others complimented her family's politeness. This was a good Saturday. The kids kissed her as she continued to do her weekly cleaning, laundry and errands and they continued with their day of leisure. The routine weekend was interrupted by a call from her friend, Dena. Dena had some concerns for which she wanted to elicit help from her friend, Mia.

Knowing that she would be exhausted if she continued on her routine weekend duties, Mia sought a reprieve from her family, who, although they showed gratitude for all that she did for them, were not accustomed to placing active motion behind the words associated with physical work. She was needed by her friend and that was a meeting of which she was not going to miss.

Dena and Mia had met through Mia's niece A.J. It was quite comical, really. Family friends met Dena, decided that she would be a good match for Mia's bachelor brother and wanted to get them together. Raymond, the intended man bait, was not the type to be blindsided by some two-legged dessert and his family was well- aware. Having been through this before, he repeatedly declined any hint of being male bait. It was not part of his personality nor his disposition to be like his siblings. He liked being the lone wolf. He was okay with being single. Enter Dena.

Dena was new to the area. She met A.J. at their place of employment, having transferred to the area roughly a year ago. From the beginning, A.J. had made the declaration that Dena would make an excellent aunt. A.J. couldn't explain why, only that Dena would fit perfectly into their wacky family.

Dena's calming, patient nature and her wickedly sharp humor fit the equation to Raymond's jovial personality.

It just so happens that the family, Mia's family, made it a point to get together on Sundays after church. A house full of family, siblings, cousins and then some. The culinary experts were in the kitchen placing final touches on the meal while complimenting each other on their dishes, the desserts, the nose-teasing fragrances and the appearances of the feast that was arranged for their viewing. Paper plates, napkins, and plastic utensils did not diminish these culinary treats! Family and togetherness: laughter and love!

What seemed to be some tribal ceremony was placed in the hands of these royal women who provided safety for the children and a place of honor for the mature. The women tended to congregate together as did the men. While this ritual in itself was impressive, the show did not begin until after dinner. Just like a Broadway show, the family's stage production was imaginative, impromptu, and hysterically educational for all.

The "I remember when" segment proved to make everyone aware of some situation, event or life milestone that the orator thought no one else was aware of. Remembering a child's view of things at the age of five or six proved priceless. "Things that I did in high school" scored high for everyone, leaving much to the imagination and a lot of mumbled, hushed voices to protect the adults from the probing questions of the kids. "Extra-curricular activities" evoked laughs and jokes as the kids made faces of amusement and bewilderment. All went silent, followed by an eruption of laughter. Somewhere during all of this, there was the first call for dessert.

Like clockwork, the female task force went to work allocating dessert for the honored mature and the young and giggly. The men, while attempting to communicate with charm and finesse, remained seated while dessert was delivered to them, again evoking laughter. The males' responses were sweet and steady as molasses dripping from their lips and as smooth as a ballad song by Luther Vandross. It was amazing how the young boys paid close attention to the adult males and the girls shifted their desserts being sure that there was enough for everyone. The children thanked the women and continued to observe the communication among the adults.

As the children observed the adults, the happiness of the family group, and the sweet comfort of the desserts, they, too, began to laugh louder and louder as they ate from each other's plates. The men, kissing the hand that provided them with a sweet end to the day and in some cases, in the gentlest of manner, kissing the mother of their children and respecting the queen of their castle.

Dena, being one of the providers of the dessert vanguard, was also met with gentle, manly bows and a kiss of the hand which she responded to with a royal tilt of her head and a mini curtsy. She fit this family. Not sure of the origin or the cohesive management of it, Dena felt as if she belonged. She no longer felt like a stranger.

For months now, Dena, Mia and A.J. had been planning the Sunday get-together with Dena participating progressively more with family favorite foods as well as favorite desserts. Other family members, particularly the women, knew Raymond and had gotten to know Dena. Dena and Raymond had inadvertently gotten to know each other, too. After months of family dating, you know, getting to know each other while in the midst of family activities, they bonded. Dena was at a crossroads. There were things that she had not told Mia. Things that Dena thought might have an impact on how Mia might perceive their friendship. Dena was looking for a way to explain things to Mia, but how would this conversation begin?

Dena; true friend, positive thinker, slightly superstitious, five-feet-five inches of trustworthiness. All synonymous with the person that Mia had been friends with for months, but now, how would Dena begin to explain herself. She could tell Mia that when she found pennies, she was happy. When she found coins, good things happened in her life. Dena could tell Mia about the time that she couldn't get the gas cap off of her car and that some guy came and removed it, without a problem, after she had tried to do so for what seemed to be forever. She saw pennies on the ground and she began to smile.

From that time on, she seemed to see coins everywhere; the gas station, the post office, the grocery store. She continued to smile and good things followed. On more than one occasion, she would accidentally see the gas-cap guy. At some point over time, their coincidental meetings found purpose.

That had been months ago. She had grown close to him and his family and friends. Maybe it was meant to be. Pennies from heaven.

Legacy
By Grant Perryman

For my children's, children's, children
Hold your head high
Like a giraffe grazing on the African plains.
Catch your dreams
Like a lioness stalking unsuspecting prey.
Aim for the sky and fly high
Like an eagle circling the Ethiopian
    mountainous terrain.
Grasp your destiny
Like a spider's web shimmering in the sun's rays.

Know this
That each day is a challenge with tears
    for tomorrow
But faith, hope and love will cover all
    your sorrows.
Rise up when you fall down
Like a newborn gazelle standing on its own.
Never give up and never quit

Like a hungry mother leopard on the prowl.
Stand your ground
Like the roots of an ancient baobab tree.
Submerge yourself in God's Holy Word
Like a hippopotamus bathing in the waters
    of the Nile.

For you are
The great descendants of Adam and Eve who
    walked in the shadows of Kilimanjaro
You are great and full of worth, with
    immeasurable value beyond tomorrow.

Her Hands Told Her Life Story

By Linda Dogue' Holliman

Her hands told her life story. She sat waiting, her chestnut-brown hands in her lap, left over right, mimicking her crossed legs, except that her left ankle was tucked behind her right. She sat quietly, no cell phone, no reading material, no game or craft project or puzzle, nor anything people commonly use to fill empty spaces of time. She simply waited, with her hands expectantly in her lap.

A muted nail color, Cherry Kiss, polished each fingertip. Her small diamond solitaire and plain gold band declared her status as a missus. Those rings once slipped on easily, but now they formed a restrictive collar. The diamond glinted in the light despite a little soap scum in the crevices of the simple setting.

Soft folds and crisscrosses of fine lines, counted her years like rings on a tree stump. Hours spent standing in front of ironing boards, cutting boards, steaming pots, and sizzling frying pans, resulted in several minor burns, and once, a deep laceration that caused shrieks followed by pressure, ice packs, and goopy applications of aloe vera gel, calendula cream, and vitamin E oil for weeks afterwards.

Hers were loyal hands, caring hands, trusting hands. Love had given her hands the joyful tasks of massaging her faithful husband's back after a hard day, of bathing and changing the sweet little babies who arrived one after another, and of later framing and hanging their high school diplomas. Honor had given her hands clothes to sew, dough to knead, and gardens to tend. Devotion had helped her hands tie shoe laces, button jackets, drive carpools, carry groceries, pack lunches, wipe away tears, turn the pages of photo albums, polish furniture, sign for deliveries, count up a week's wages, pick up suits from the dry cleaners, and send college care packages.

Faith had helped her hands scribble in her journal, hold her weary head, and pray her desires to God. Hope had helped her hands gather the makings of a sparse yet nutritious dinner, and then in the lateness of the same evening, open bedroom doors to check on slumbering heads poking out from warm blankets covering satisfied tummies.

"Number seventy-three!" She was next. Her hands dug into her purse, and reemerged gripping some papers. And then she slowly walked toward the next chapter of her life story.

The Crossing
By Steven R. Butler

You've walked with her for ever so many miles
Along the banks of that rushing river,
Not noticing the speed at which
Time had passed you by;
The sparkling sunlight in her hair
And the warm sand you've felt gently between
    your toes.
The love and the joy that you shared,
The peaceful solitude unending and so sublime;
But as the sun sinks in the distance
And you stand there in your sorrow,
Parting is your inevitable fate.
The embrace you have shared must end,
And the rushing river, you must cross.
Slowly into the shallows you trod.
You turn back as she stands there on the shore,
Her face streaked with tears,
But nothing can stop you, the rapids
    swallow you up;

Tumbling, churning, helter-skelter
Through the cold, dark, tearing current
Until suddenly a snag, something solid, a rock you
    can grasp;
And wearily, worn, torn, and shivering, you
Pull yourself through the darkness,
You find the opposite bank; you drag your
    tired frame,
Cut and bleeding, knarled and sore, you
Tumble to the ground on the other shore.
Alone and spent, you gather yourself together,
Knowing that you have
Made it to the other side......

The Mewsings of Detective Stewie
By Anita L. Robertson

With his eyes partially closed, Detective Stewie squatted, his legs hidden beneath his body and his arms curled under his chest, creating the deception that he was comfortably oblivious to his surroundings while he was catnapping. But really, he was busy contemplating all the angles of the mystery. It was only when a slight sound reached his ears that one could see evidence of his keen and active mind. For upon hearing such sound, he would open his eyes, assess the situation, and quickly shut them again, resuming his analytical thoughts.

Today Detective Stewie sat especially perplexed. Being a perpetual student of body language, he was drawn to the mystery of the Mona Lisa smile and never leaving a cat kibble unturned, he decided he needed to get down to the bottom of the bowl. So, with his eyes closed he recited the special cat purr sequence, put himself in Zen mode, and telepathically travelled back in time to the year 1503, to visit Leonardo da Vinci. "Poor Albert Einstein," Stewie had mused. "He could only theorize about time travel, and having only touched the tip of the cat's tail, could not even begin to understand the application."

Upon opening his eyes, Detective Stewie was pleased to find himself "perched" on a rafter in a corner of Leonardo's art studio in Florence, Italy. Music was quietly playing and from his vantage point he could see out a large, open window overlooking a vineyard: the glorious sunlight leaving the landscape in a whitewash of gold. Looking back into the room and to his right was Leonardo's mixing area, complete with tools, where the artist painstakingly ground his pigments. On the bench were several canisters containing paints of various shades of blue, gray and brown. In the corner on the floor on the other side of the window were two of Leonardo's works. One, a personal favorite of Stewie's, was an older painting entitled "Madonna with the Cat". He felt that Leonardo had done justice to the feline persuasion by putting the cat where it rightfully belonged. The second was a sketch that Detective Stewie could never figure out. What on earth would possess Leonardo to draw a man with multiple limbs? And trapped in a circle, no less. Surely Leonardo could see humans only have two arms and two legs and don't live in circles, although it would be in a cat's best interest for a human to have more hands to pet with.

To the right of the center was Leonardo, standing with his back to Stewie, easel in one hand and paintbrush in the other. An older gentleman, his genius appearing to flow out of his long gray hair and beard, down his arm and onto the poplar canvas. It was an invigorating sight to see, for Leonardo stood like a god, his hand first dancing passionately over the canvas in front of him and then lessening quickly to such minute strokes that his fingers appeared stationary. So inspired by the master, Detective Stewie thought for a moment that he might just pursue this hobby when he returned home. Maybe he would paint Leonardo!

And there, across from Leonardo, sat an exuberant Mona Lisa herself. She was all dressed in black and she looked about twenty-five years old, although it was hard to tell on account of the mathematics involved in the cat to human age ratio not being a constant. Leonardo was painting her in a half-length portrait, the style of which no one had ever done before. No doubt, he was doing this to include the beautiful white Persian cat who was curled up comfortably asleep on Mona Lisa's lap. Suddenly noticing the greyhound sprawled at her feet, Detective Stewie was momentarily seized by panic and thought he might fall off the rafters and lose one of his nine lives, but he came to the realization that he could not have fallen off as he was there in spirit only and he chuckled to himself, resuming his vigilance.

"La Giaconda, is there any particular reason your husband commissioned me to paint your portrait?" Leonardo asked in the most beautiful Italian.

"He has long been an admirer of your talent and decided that to celebrate the completion of our new home and the pending birth of our child, now would be the best time to have my portrait done," she enthusiastically replied.

As all cats are linguistically brilliant, and know every language ever spoken, Detective Stewie had no problem following the Italian conversation. One can see this when a human compliments a cat in any language and the cat will always respond in an affectionate way.

"My husband is currently away buying silk in China, and when he returns and sells it, he should make a nice profit. I should love to buy a cat such as this one," she said, looking at the cat with longing.

"With profits, you will be able to buy a fine cat," he followed, though confused by the sadness over-coming her face.

"No, I cannot. Francesco will not allow me to keep such an animal. He does not want their fur or their fleas on his merchandise." She looked about to cry and Detective Stewie's heart melted, as he thought that this was the type of woman who was truly deserving of a cat's company. Leonardo, not knowing how to soothe her, nervously set down his brush, accidentally dropping it on the floor, which so jarred the greyhound that he jumped up and woofed. This in turn so startled the cat, that she jumped off Mona Lisa's lap, ran to the open window, and jumped out. Detective Stewie watched in a state of perspicacity while Leonardo immediately collected the unstable animal.

No wonder Leonardo did not want him in the picture, thought Stewie. Further proof that cats are far more civilized.

Leonardo, having left the room abruptly, returned quickly with a goblet of water for his young subject. She thanked him, took a sip and handed the goblet back.

"Would you prefer to come back tomorrow?" Leonardo inquired.

"It is unlikely the cat should come back tomorrow as it has had an excessive fright, so it is better if we continue," she said, deflated.

Leonardo picked his brush up off the floor, and concluding it unsatisfactory to work with, replaced it with another. He stood for a few minutes, frustrated and debating his conundrum when he looked up at Lisa, who had settled serenely back into her armchair. Her previously bright smile, was now replaced by a sorrowful yet tranquil expression. Leonardo was enchanted.

"Please, bella, do not think of anything else. Freeze your thoughts. Your face is exquisite right now. Do not move," he implored. Obliging, she remained still while Leonardo took her arms gently and positioned them where the cat had been. He would have to repaint her, but this would be better.

Detective Stewie's investigation had now come to an end. Although he wanted to chew the catnip for a while and enjoy Florence, he worried that his human would need him, so he reversed the time travel trajectory and ended up back home, back in his body.

After coming to an indisputable conclusion about the origin of Mona Lisa's smile, Detective Stewie sprang up and mimicked the famous Halloween cat stretch to relieve his body of the tension created by sitting motionless for hours. Looking around to see if anyone was watching—if there wasn't, he would do it anyway to keep his skills sharp—he would proceed in a methodical manner to lick his right paw with utmost attention to detail, starting on the outside, then moving toward the inside. Using one quick move, he would switch to his left paw without paying heed to onlookers, so as to keep them fully absorbed in his red herring of grooming narcissism. The goal was to give the illusion that he was all about his good looks and didn't have anything between his ears. But if you looked carefully in his eyes, you could catch him laughing every time he did this maneuver, because it has fooled humans for centuries. Clever cat!

Life Is Too Short
By La'Neisha Kennedy

Life is too short
For all the lying, crying, fighting
I don't want to fight
I don't like to fight
Life is too short to fight
When we fight it makes me want
You out of my life
Out of my sight
Life is too short to wonder where we might
    separate or
Depart
But I can't get you out of my heart
Yet and still I will not tolerate unhappiness
Cause without happiness my life is a mess
Sometimes I wonder
Is it all a test
And will it work out for the best

I love my life
And I refuse to live the rest of my life
Selling myself short
Because Life Is Too Short.

I Love You
By Nina Pringle

Dedicated to my children and the Youth at
New Testament Holy Church of Jesus

I may not know you, but I love you. I love you with
the love of God. I know my love does not compare
to the love God and his Son, Jesus Christ, have for
you. God is love, Jesus is the personification of God,
and I am his humble servant. God has allowed me
to receive a portion of His great love and I want to
share it with you from my heart.

The most quoted and familiar scripture of the
Bible says, **"For God so loved the world, that
He gave his only begotten son, that whosoever
believeth in him should not perish, but have
everlasting life."** (John 3:16) God so loved us that
he sent his son Jesus Christ to die for our sins that
we may have eternal life in him. I want to help you
receive eternal life.

I have observed the people in my life and I know they can live a better and happier life. I know what they are seeking can't be found in the things and the people that they are seeking after. We all need a relationship with God and that is what they are seeking after and just don't know it. God is our creator; we have an inherent need for a relationship with him. Until we develop that relationship with God we will continue to look in all the wrong places for what we need. God has given explicit instructions in the Bible on how to receive Him and eternal life and He has sent many men of the gospel to teach us His will.

God's will for our life is for us to love him with all of our heart, mind, soul, and strength. Until we find Jesus we are in a lost state of sin. This may sound foreign, but trust me, it is real. Heaven and Hell are real and we will have to go to one or the other one day. Why not make a conscious choice where to spend eternity? You may not fully believe in God, Heaven, Hell, or the ever after, but are you willing to take that kind of chance with your life, forever? If there is a chance that you can live a better life here, now, wouldn't it be worth your consideration to try and find out how to do that?

When I took heed to the word of God, I started to understand life and why I am here on earth. I didn't find true meaning in life and happiness until I got married and my husband introduced me to the Lord. It wasn't a tragedy or a horrible life that brought me to faith as is the case with so many. I received deliverance and salvation by way of acceptance. I had

bar

grace it caused every human being of his decent to be conceived in sin. From the fall of Adam up until now, the hearts of men have become filled with evil. So many people have turned away from God that this world is in a place that is far worse than it was when God destroyed it the first time (Noah's day). I believe the words that are written in the Bible and I believe that God is grieved and so sickened with how Satan has captivated the minds of the people that it won't be too much longer before God destroys this earth again. We have heard for years that God is coming soon. *Soon*, may not be in my lifetime or yours, but whenever He does destroy the world, it will be too soon. The real issue for us is that we don't know what hour or day we will die and leave this earth. So beloved one, get your soul right with the Lord now.

God has given us every opportunity to surrender our lives to him and has laid a clear path for us to receive salvation. I am so grateful and blessed to have found the truth. I am trying to help you understand this world is not our home and that God has prepared a beautiful place for us to spend eternity.

Young people nowadays seem to have lost all consciousness about the way they live their lives. Satan has really deceived people into believing that: Same-sex relationships/marriage is okay; pre-marital sex is acceptable; adultery is acceptable; the use of drugs and alcohol is acceptable. It is not, beloved ones, God is not pleased with the way we are living our lives. God said for us to live holy in this present world and we can do it, beloved one. The scripture says, **"I can do all things through Christ which strengtheneth me."** (Philippians 4:13) If God said for us to live holy then we can live holy. All we have to do is make up our mind and seek the help of the Lord. He will send someone into our life that will teach us and encourage us to live the best life that we can live in Christ Jesus. I wouldn't tell you to do something that I did not feel possible, but because I have done it and do it every day. I know that you too can do it. Believe that it is possible. Believe that we serve a God that has all power in His hands and made Heaven and Earth and all that is therein.

He can cause us to live holy and sanctified if we want to in this present world amongst all that is going on in the world. All that we have to do is put our faith and belief into action. It really is that easy; believe and trust God to lead you to a better life in Christ Jesus. I promise it will be the single most important thing that you have ever done or will ever do in your life. You may make a mistake, but as long as you follow His commandments, which He says, **"are not grievous"** (1 John 5:3) and love him with all of your heart, you are living a holy, saved, sanctified life in Jesus.

The majority of the human race will believe whatever they are taught, which is why so many people are lost and gone astray. Study God's word for yourself. Don't solely rely on what the preacher says or someone else you think knows what they are talking about says. You cannot be influenced by God's word if you do not spend adequate time reading His Word.

Please don't think that you are too young to devote your life to the Lord. If you are young, strong, and vibrant you are just right for God to use you to influence other young people. I understand that you might feel like you are giving up everything or that you won't be able to have any fun, or that you won't be able to hang out with your friends. I know how you feel, of course, I know that sin is fun. It's the devil's job to make it fun and enticing. I've been there, at times it was fun, the problem is that the fun never lasted and at times it was even dangerous. I don't miss anything about the world or the lustful things/people that I engaged in. The life that I live now is far more enjoyable and blessed! Peace of mind is difficult to find or have in this world we live in. I see so many young people, including my own children, who seem so unhappy, stressed out, depressed, lost, etc., because they are searching for Jesus in all the wrong places. They love the world and the things that are in the world instead of loving God who made the world and them.

The word of God is true and God is real and he is coming back one day for His saints and I want to be one that He receives into His Kingdom. I pray and hope that you will be received also! I cannot say enough that, "I love you" and that I want you to be saved from this world of sin and destruction. We are living in the worst generation of all time: Same-sex marriage has been legalized and now marijuana is legal. There is not too much more that Satan can bring to this world that hasn't been done already, just more of it. You don't have to be caught up in all of it. God is a refuge in a time of trouble; a present help in a time of need.

Your peace of mind and health is something that you shouldn't compromise for anyone or anything. You can love and be truly loved by God and your peers if you allow God to live in you. Once you receive God into your heart and start living out His plan, you will be ever so grateful. There is no amount of alcohol or drugs that can give you a feeling like receiving the Holy Spirit. God will fill your life with everything and everyone that you need to be happy and at peace.

God has given me so much peace and contentment; my life has been filled in every aspect. If I were to die today, I have no complaints. God loves you no matter what you have done or what you are doing in your life right now. He will forgive you of all of your sins. 1 John 1:9 says, **"If we confess our sins, he is faithful and just to forgive us our sins, and to cleanse us from all unrighteousness."**

You may think that no one will ever love you or that you can't be loved. That is not true. God loves you no matter what! I love you—that's why I am reaching out to you right now. I want you to be at peace in your mind and live a life full of joy. Matthew 24 lets us know that time is winding up and Satan knows that too, so he is moving rampantly. You don't have to be one of Satan's victims. You can be one of God's victors! It's up to you! My heart's desire is that you will understand this message that I am trying to convey to you because it is a matter of life and death. It doesn't end here beloved one. I love you. But the real question is: Do you love you? If you do, please receive my plea, and surrender your all to the Lord!

Please read: Ephesians 4:22-32; Titus 2:11-14; 1 John 3:1-10; and 1 John 4:7-12.

Scotti Butler is a California girl, born in 1936; she is a retired you-name-it living in a quirky house in Vallejo where she cohabits with her quirky husband, Steven, a quirky Jack Russell mixed terrier named, Tootsie, a very large Maine Coon cat named, Tracker, and a somewhat skittish Siamese-mix cat named, Punkins.

Scotti focuses her writing in the areas of memoir, poetry and perspectives. A self-styled late bloomer, Scotti is looking forward to having more of her memoirs and perspectives published soon. Readers can correspond with Scotti at aquariesb@aol.com.

Steven Butler is a third generation native of California, having lived most of his life in the picturesque Napa Valley, as well as several communities in Northern California. Steven wrote his first short story at age 9 and published his first work in the Petaluma Argus Courier at age 12. His experience at a San Francisco Giants baseball game won his first award for fiction writing in eighth grade at age 14. Steven loves writing about his experiences growing up in the Napa Valley, as well as spinning romantic and science fiction tales set in his Northern California home. Steven can be reached at wease01@aol.com

Wanda B. Campbell resides in the San Francisco Bay Area with her family. She proudly balances the roles of wife, mother, grandmother, minister, mentor, teacher, author, public health care worker, and college student. Wanda began writing in 2006, and currently has 12 published Christian Fiction novels. She has appeared on multiple best-selling lists and won various recognitions for her nontraditional edgy writing style. Wanda's passion is motivating others to fulfill their dreams and to pursue their passion. Learn more about Wanda's work at www. wandabcampbell.com or join her Facebook group: Wanda B. Campbell Readers and Supporters.

Naomi Connor is a wife, mother and author. She is married to a retired military member and is a volunteer who, until recently, focused writing children's books of which she has four to her credit. Aside from the short stories that are included in this anthology, she is anticipating a writing change and welcomes the opportunity to show her southern, relatively comical side to an otherwise quiet personality. She can be contacted at fnconnor@comcast.net.

Rita "em" Emery currently resides in Northern California with her two cats, Kasha and Scruffy.

She received her Bachelor and Master's degrees in Education, Health Education, and Recreation. She is a retired, private, public and collegiate, teacher, mentor, and coach who is a life-long fitness buff along with being an avid sports fan. Presently, she spends her time volunteering at the Suisun Wildlife Center and traveling.

Grant Hayden Holliman combines insight and humor in his oral and written musings. Otherwise ordinary observations reveal sometimes shocking surprises when Grant puts his pen to the page.

A recent high school graduate, Grant designs and manufactures custom 3D models using computer-aided design (CAD) software. He is also a popular portrait and event photographer.

Grant Hayden Holliman can be reached by email at noahsbrownboat@outlook.com.

Linda Dogué Holliman explores the marriage relationship, family life, and the adventurous journey of childhood with her pen. Her husband of over 25 years, and their two sons, provide much of her inspiration. "God blesses our family every day, and we are grateful."

Ms. Holliman earned her bachelor's degree in Art History from Stanford University. She has taught craft-making and visual arts, as well as creative writing and poetry to students of all ages.

Linda Dogué Holliman can be reached by email at lydiaspurpletext@live.com.

Eddrick Jerome grew up in the San Francisco Bay Area and developed his passion for writing as a young child. His first book of short stories, *Grippings*, was self-published in1997. Eddrick has spent the past several years focused on family and career and has recently rekindled his love for writing. His primary literary influences are Chester Himes and Henry Miller. Eddrick loves listening to music and is a big fan of Prince, The Roots, and Robert Glasper.

Eddrick can be contacted via email at 3mel@ phatbooks.com

LaNeisha Kennedy is the mother of two beautiful daughters, and also a grandmother. LaNeisha was born and raised in Richmond, California, where she excelled in Stepping, theater, dancing, and pageants. Her occupation as a hairstylist exposed her to the world of modeling, fashion and entertainment. LaNeisha's unique creative hair-braiding styles have been featured on several runways. She enjoys photography as a hobby, and in her spare time, writes poems and songs.

Ruth LaMell is a resident of Fairfield, California. She is the proud mother of two sons, and three grandchildren. Ruth's yearning to write began at the age of ten. Ruth is a longtime WRC member, and published her first book in 2011.

Janell Michael has written many short stories over the past twenty years. You can read some of her work in *Inspire Christian Writers' Love Anthology* and in *Stories of Faith and Courage from Prison.* Janell's first collection of retold fairytales titled, *Fairytales Redeemed – A Women's Study on the Power of Love, Forgiveness and Reconciliation* will be released the summer of 2018.

C.L. Miles was born in Santa Cruz, California, where she joined the Air Force serving her country as a Security Police/Law Enforcement NCO honorably. As a disabled veteran she received an AA degree in Child Development. When not writing, she enjoys spending time with her children and grandchild. She also writes under the pen name CL Garland and would love to hear from you at milescindy0@gmail.com.

Roger Oberbeck is an Electrical Engineer with a BSEE degree from the University of Wisconsin. He served in the U.S. Navy as an Electronics Technician on Aircraft Carriers Wasp and Point Cruz. He worked as a Guided Missile Systems Field Engineer; as a Nuclear Chief Test Engineer and Nuclear Information Manager at Mare Island Naval Shipyard; and as a Biotech/Pharmaceutical Validation Engineer. He lives near Fairfield, California with his wife Conny; son Brandon; wild Mustangs Talitha and Raphael; German Shepard Bruno; Chihuahua Chauncey; and cats Meshach and Shadrach.

Grant Perryman was born to read. Reading empowered his imagination to travel around the world. In 7th grade, Grant, wrote his first poem influenced by the legends of the Harlem Renaissance. He found his voice through the likes of Claude McKay, Langston Hughes and Nikki Giovanni just to name a few. Grant's expanding repertoire includes several Christian- based theatrical plays, which is how he met his wife of 14 years. He also became writer and editor of *Five Years to Life*, a prison ministry newsletter. He has written his first children's book titled, *Ama's Dream*, which will be published later this year.

Nina P. Pringle was born in Erin, Tennessee in 1960 and moved to Oakland, California at the age of 8 years old. Being the fifth of twelve children, Nina was raised with great family values that enabled her to be a good mother and wife. In 1982, Nina married a wonderful man, and they have three beautiful children and six grandchildren. Nina has served the Lord for the past 36 years, and is now looking for the Lord to bless her in her Ministry and writing. You may contact Nina via e-mail at Nppringle@comcast.net or Holycdr@comcast.net

Anita L. Robertson was born in Canada, to Latvian immigrants. She was raised in Ontario and received a diploma in Radiography, and a Bachelors of Science in Wildlife Biology, before moving to the United States. She has resided in the San Francisco Bay Area for over 18 years, with her husband, four children, a dog and several rescued cats. She can be reached at author.anitar@gmail.com.

Patricia Vincent is the mother of three children and lives in the San Francisco Bay Area. Having grown up in the Bay Area, Patricia received secondary education and vocational training throughout Contra Costa and Solano Counties. Her training and experiences have afforded her the opportunity to work with service organizations such as, The School for the Blind and the Boy Scouts of America.

Patricia would love to hear your feedback at pepperlk7171@gmail.com.

Vicki L. Ward has written five books; three have won multiple awards. Her titles include: *Life's Spices From Seasoned Sistahs; A Collection of Life Stories from Mature Women of Color* used in Women's Studies courses; *Savvy, Sassy and Bold After 50: A Midlife Rebirth,* and *Savvy, Sassy and Bold After 50 Workbook; More of Life Spices; Seasoned Sistahs Keepin' It Real, Supercharge Your Life After 60; 10 Tips to Navigate A Dynamic Decade* a resource for managing life changes for seniors and aging parents. Vicki is retired, a full-time writer and publisher. Her short stories and poetry have appeared in many anthologies.

Vicki can be contacted via her website, Facebook or Twitter.

Website: http://vickiward.net/blog/
Facebook: https://www.facebook.com/SeasonedSistahs/
Twitter: https://twitter.com/@seasonedsistah2

Carl Weber is a Graduate of Old Dominion University, Norfolk, Virginia with a B.A. in English. Carl started writing poetry as a teenager. As he grew older, Carl moved away from poetry to free verse and prose. Today, his writing appears as blogs on the human condition. Carl's desire is to write a book filled with pieces on how we live and think. Though he may appear opinionated, Carl's works will present questions and ask readers to find answers within themselves as to the destiny of the human race. Readers can contact Carl at orionxxxnow@gmail.com.

Alan Werblin was born in New York and raised in New Jersey. He attended Yale University, where he studied Psychology, Philosophy, Music, and African-American culture. He then moved to California and played harmonica in blues bands.

After working as an orderly on the county psychiatric wards, Alan graduated from UCSF Medical School and University of Miami Family Medicine Residency Program. He practiced

Family Medicine at Kaiser Clinics in Fairfield and Vacaville, CA, for 26 years. Alan became a Christian in 1995.

He currently enjoys playing his harmonica, working part-time as a physician, and spending time with his wife, children and grandchildren.

Carole Williams-Morrison resides in Northern California with her husband. She is a retired public school teacher, a mother and grandmother. She draws upon her growing up years in Georgia to tell true stories of the people she loved and their struggles to survive adversity.

Carole can be reached via e-mail: cmorri4036@ aol.com

CPSIA information can be obtained
at www.ICGtesting.com
Printed in the USA
FSHW01n1320031018
52694FS